THE DARK TRAIL
TO NOWHERE

Lucas Santana is a freelance range detective — and a wanted man in some states — who has several aliases; nor is he shy about lining his own pockets in order to finance his Wyoming ranch. When a number of gold coins surface in South Texas, loot from a big heist years back, both Pinkerton and the US Marshals call on his services to find their source. Problem is, Santana's not the only one searching for it — and when a fellow agent is murdered in cold blood, his quest becomes personal . . .

HARRY JAY THORN

THE DARK TRAIL TO NOWHERE

Complete and Unabridged

LINFORD
Leicester

First published in Great Britain in 2017 by
Robert Hale
an imprint of The Crowood Press
Wiltshire

First Linford Edition
published 2020
by arrangement with
The Crowood Press
Wiltshire

A catalogue record for this book is available
from the British Library.

ISBN 978–1–4448–4533–4

Published by
Ulverscroft Limited
Anstey, Leicestershire

Set by Words & Graphics Ltd.
Anstey, Leicestershire
Printed and bound in Great Britain by
T. J. International Ltd., Padstow, Cornwall

This book is printed on acid-free paper

Prologue

New Orleans 1875

It was raining; it usually was in New Orleans, especially at that time of the year. On the outside the rainwater ran down the single window of my office, while on the inside, via a leak in the ceiling, into a wooden bucket. I had just emptied the bucket of rainwater when he burst in through the doorway, came in like a whirlwind, a big man in an ill-fitting grey town suit, a dark-skinned man, a ''breed' I suspected, as wide as he was tall. But the big body carried a very small head on which sat an undersized black derby hat. He plonked himself down on the old barroom chair in front of my desk and wriggled his way down between the narrow arms to the seat. It was a tight fit and I wondered would he ever be able to get up out of it. He stared at me long and hard, sizing me up, his lips tightly pursed. He had obsidian black eyes that roamed beyond me to the wall behind my desk upon which I had hung two large portraits — one of General Robert E. Lee and the other of General Ulysses S. Grant, both in the uniforms of their respective armies. I tried not to play favourites and to accommodate all. He switched his gaze from them to the one spare chair — sometimes clients came in pairs — then down at his chair, then at my chair. His black eyes took in the large wooden filing cabinet, which was empty apart from three stolen shot glasses and a half-full or, depending on your point of view, a half-empty fifth of Scotch. The cabinet was merely a prop to show how busy I was. He glanced at the door that led to the small washroom, shifting his gaze up to the empty hat rack — I seldom remove my hat during waking hours — and finally back to me. Staring hard, thinking.

'You have to help me,' he said quietly. 'I heard you are good at helping people and I need help real bad.' His voice was nut-brown, tobacco-stained, deep, dark like his eyes.

'How can I be of help, Mister . . . ?' I asked, keeping my voice low, not wanting to agitate the big man.

'Darryl J. Jones, but just Jones will do. Some folk call me Jonesy.'

'OK, so how can I be of help, Mr Jones?'

'They are trying to rob me, steal my bar from under me.'

'Who would that be and where is your bar exactly?'

As I waited, I fished out the makings from my vest pocket, stripped a Rizla from the back of the sack and rolled a neat quirly, tossing the Durham onto the desk in front of him, but he shook his head.

'The Lucky Dollar on the south side of the tracks,' he said.

Below the line, I thought, *not a place a man wanted to go if he had gold teeth or a decent pocket watch on view.* I waited for more.

'They are the people you did a job for some time back. They call themselves the Saloon Owners Syndicate and they want to own both sides of the line.'

'They offer you a fair price for the saloon?' I asked.

He gave me a grim smile and a one-word answer. 'No.'

I waited some more. I always find it best to let an angry man talk himself out rather than act out.

'You did a job for them. I heard they like you, is that right?'

'The first part, yes. I do not know about the second part though. They never told me they liked me; all I did was collect some money they were owed.'

'You're their dog.'

'No, Jones, I am nobody's dog,' I said.

He reached inside his long frock suit coat and took out a large bladed Bowie knife, leaned forward and stabbed it hard into the desk top. The force of the strike sank the blade a good three inches into the hard wood surface. I reached across the desk and gave it a tug, anxious to show I was not easily intimidated, but the blade stuck fast and would need a young King Arthur to remove it. (I am a well-read man.)

He was silent for a while, thinking again, his narrow brow furrowed beneath the tight brim of the derby.

I tried to ignore the knife and shrugged, letting it sit there between us throwing a cross-like shadow from the afternoon sun on the far wall. It had stopped raining and the sun was shining once again on Bourbon Street. The gin joints would open, the music would soon begin and the streets throng with people. I smiled and leaned back in my chair, uncertain as to what would come next, but happy with the fact that, unlike my normal habit of removing my weapon when in the office, I had kept the high-ride holster and Colt on my hip. Pulling from a sitting position is not easy, but I was well practised in the art. I waited.

'They are trying to wear me down,

scare me out. They killed my dog.' A sudden softening of his tone — he was thinking again. Staring at the portraits, I wasn't sure which of the two he liked the best.

'Have you been to the law?' I asked.

'Their law? The inspector told me I needed cast iron proof. Sent me to a lawyer, a shyster.'

'And?'

'He told me the same thing and that proving it would prove costly. They wreck my place regularly. I'm losing customers, and I can't afford to go to court, their court, their cops, their shyster lawyer.'

'You want me to look into it?' I asked.

'You cost money as well.'

'What do you want of me then, Mr Jones?'

He reached under the left arm of his long jacket and pulled out a handsome blue-framed, snub-nosed single action Colt .38 Sheriff's revolver and pointed it at my chest.

'They killed my dog so I will kill one of theirs, does that seem fair to you?'

The gun was not cocked. In my long years as a detective, I had never been confronted by an angry client in my own office; it was something new. I eased my weight gently to my left buttock and waited. He cocked the revolver and I pulled and shot him twice in the chest, sending him and the chair over backwards. His bullet thumped into the portrait of Bobbie Lee and I took that as some kind of sign. I had worn the butternut grey for five long, bloody years. I moved quickly around the desk and kicked his smoking gun to one side and knelt beside him, wondering how I would ever get him out of the chair. He was still alive. I cradled his head on my arm.

'They killed my dog . . . ' His lips were flecked with blood, his voice trailed and faded to a murmur, any other words he had wished to say lost for all time.

I held him that way until the light faded from his eyes and he stared into the big darkness, the big darkness that comes to us all.

That was a long time ago, that rain-soaked sunny day when a half-breed named Darryl J. Jones, a man sometimes known as Jonesy, died on my office floor. I do not know Darryl's story; it could be true that the New Orleans suits were either trying to buy him out or drive him out. It was not beyond them. It was true of the south, the north and the west, where the big absentee businessmen from the east were taking over every small outfit they could. In the north it was the timber, in the south and the west the gold mines or the cattle ranches. They may even have resorted to shooting his dog. All I know for sure is that if there is a man in front of me with a cocked weapon and I can see a round in the chamber, I pull and I shoot to kill. He wasn't the first man I killed and I knew he would not be the last, but there was something about the man that reached out to me. Something that defined me, shaped me into being what I am become. I did not know then that sometime in my future Darryl Jones, the man some called Jonesy, would reach out to me from the past and from that big darkness steady my hand and save my life.

It took a five-pound hammer and a lot of muscle to remove his Bowie knife from my desk and an hour for two Orleans Parish deputies to free his body from the stout old barroom chair. In the end they had to break off the arm rests. They let me keep his Colt and shoulder rig by way of damages. I still have it and wear it sometimes when discretion is called for. Times have changed since then though. I moved on soon after that day and we no longer call a man a ''breed' — we call them people of mixed race.

1

The Wolver and the Wildcat

New Orleans was seven years ago and I have been around the dance floor a time or two since then. Seven years almost to the day and I have never forgotten Darryl J. Jones and that damp office in New Orleans. Things are different for me now, though. My office is six hundred acres of prime grazing land with its own small mountain, scattered woodland, water and a mountain lion.

You may have heard of me, Lucas Santana. If not then you have probably come across my likeness on a wanted poster in your County Sheriff's office or US Marshal's office, the latter less likely as the Federal Government tolerates me simply because I am occasionally of use to them and they are happy for me to be out there where the action is, doing their dirty work maybe, but without the protection of a badge or federal warrant. The likeness on the most recent dodger isn't too shabby. I have a bit of a beard now to go with the moustache and the black high-crowned derby hat was borrowed from the jailer and not quite my usual style, but I kept it anyway. I generally prefer lighter headgear but you get the idea, oh, and under that hat my hair is no longer dark, more peppered with grey. Well that is to be expected, given the life I lead — that and the fact that I'm closing in on being forty-five years old. They always get the height wrong, though; I am not six foot, never have been, just a tad over five ten. I look a little taller than that because I am lean, a bit gangly, and I do not ride high horses. The shorter the pony, the taller the man, and I find a Morgan suits me fine.

I had been back on my Wildcat ranch for just over two weeks and I was already feeling a little restless. More than happy to be home with Annie

Blue, but tired of the daily routine. Working the land was hard work. I was crossing the paddock of the old line shack, heading for home after a long day digging post holes, when I heard a single gunshot, not too far off; the flat crack of a high-powered rifle, a Sharps probably. I turned the Morgan's head toward the sound and made towards it. I found a clearing in the trees by some large boulders know as Willard's Rocks. I do not know why that was their given name. A man was standing in the open space where I had felled some ponderosa pine the previous fall, a tall man with a shaggy unkempt beard and teeth blackened by strong coffee and chewing tobacco. He wore a grey duster, a crumpled wide-brimmed hat, filthy whipcord pants and down-at-heel boots and carried a Sharps buffalo gun at the trail. He was standing over the body of a large cougar, its yellow fur ripped apart and bloody behind the left shoulder. He looked up and smiled as I pushed the Morgan forward and reined

13

her in close to him.

'Hi,' he said, his voice scratchy, tobacco-hoarse.

I nodded. 'You shoot that cougar, mister?' I asked.

'I sure enough did,' he said. 'Big sonofabitch ain't he just?'

'Why did you shoot it?' I asked, leaning on the saddle's pommel and looking down at the dead animal.'

'Why?'

'Yes, why? Are you going to eat it?'

'Eat it, are you crazy?' He looked puzzled. 'I'm not going to eat a damned cougar.'

'So why did you shoot it, you going to skin it?' I asked.

'Maybe, but I don't believe so, could be I might sell the head as a trophy to some easterner.'

'So, let me get this straight, you shot the cat just because it was a cat?'

'Right on, done the property owner a big favour.' He looked pleased with his answer.

'Say it was his pet cat, this property owner's?' I asked, patting the Morgan's neck; the animal was fidgeting, disturbed by the smell of the dead cat's blood. 'He may not be so pleased.'

'Who the hell has a pet mountain lion in cow country?' he said, irritation creeping into his rasping voice.

'I do,' I said. 'Or rather did have. It's a she and her name is, or rather was, Cleopatra.'

'You a crazy man?' His long rifle barrel shifted just an inch or two upwards.

'That buff gun points in my direction, you will be as dead as that cat,' I said, very quietly.

The muzzle dropped.

He looked down at the big cat and then back at me. 'What's it to you anyway?' he asked, uncertainty in his voice, the smile completely gone from his face.

'Do you have permission to shoot over this property?' I asked.

'I don't need no permission to shoot a cat on anyone's land, this is open range.'

'You do on this property,' I said. 'It's not open range and it's posted.'

'Says who?'

'I do,' I said, enjoying his growing discomfort.

'And you are?'

'I am the gunfighter, the shootist, the *pistolero*, that mad dog killer the Peaceful River Kid.'

He paled and his hand on the gun stock trembled, but I had enjoyed myself enough and maybe in some small way done a service to the magnificent animal this scum had killed for no other reason than for the pleasure it gave him. 'One more thing,' I said, 'you set down that rifle with great care and you hightail it clear off this property. I catch you anywhere near to Wildcat again and I will put your lights out, permanent, maybe skin you and tack your hide on my barn door.'

He was shaking, but did as he was asked.

'You wouldn't do that over a dead cat.' He did not sound certain of that fact. 'Sharps don't come cheap. That piece cost me lot of money.'

'I'll treasure it always then,' I said.

'What about my mule back there in the trees?'

'I have no use for a mule, so I will send it along. It will probably find its way home or I may just shoot it for the fun of it, the way you shot my cat. Now scoot.'

I watched as he took off through trees at a fast walk, heading for my stone boundary marker, and I could not resist the temptation. I pulled my Colt and put two rounds close to his boot heels. He sped up some after that.

I buried the mountain lion I had known as Cleo where she lay beneath the aspens by the big rocks. I buried her in a shallow grave and built a cairn of stones over her, tipped my hat to her memory and headed for home, thinking the mountain and the Wildcat would be a lesser place without her.

★　★　★

'You look pleased with yourself, Lucas. What have you been up to?'

Annie Blue and her soft, rich voice, the love of my life. I pulled her to me, kissed her gently, ran my fingers through her lush black hair and said, 'Just riding fences and the cattle, checking the boundaries, boring stuff like that, like I did yesterday and the day before that and the day before that.'

In fact, I was feeling rather pleased with myself. I had made a head tally and figured we had two hundred head of beef. Not a lot but enough for one man to handle and come next spring there would be maybe fifty more.

'Humph,' she said, giving me that smile that always made me wonder why I spent so much time away from her. 'You have been back home two weeks and you're bored already? Are you also in trouble? Gus Street was by here this morning heading for his spread. Said he will be back this evening, so I invited him for supper. That OK with you?'

'Sure enough,' I said. I liked Gus

Street, Blackwater County's sheriff; we went fishing for rainbow trout together sometimes on the nearby narrow backwater of the Blackwater River, a run-off from the Wind River, the clear, clean water running fast through the rocky foothills of the Big Horn Mountains.

'What did the old coot want?'

'He didn't say, but I got the feeling it was something he was none too happy about. There, talk of the devil, I think I see him.'

Annie Blue was part Teton Sioux, one of the Lakota Group of the Sioux Nation who whipped Custer in '76 up north in Montana along the Greasy Grass River. A sharp-eyed woman, her mother a sub chief's daughter and her father a proud cavalry officer from New England where she was born, loved and raised more than a decade before Custer's last stand, sometimes referred to as a massacre. It wasn't; it was a fight and we lost. She was right and a few minutes later Street's tall in the saddle figure was clear to the both of us.

'I'll go inside and make some coffee. Leave you two to whatever it is you talk about when I am not around.' She slapped my behind and hustled back inside.

Gus rode an unusually large buckskin mare, a horse I coveted. I had tried to buy her from him on several occasions, but he had always declined the offer, asking why I wanted her when he knew I preferred the smaller Morgan. I told him I just wanted her on my range so's I could admire her, not ride her.

He reined in close to the house, dismounted with a groan, led the animal to the metal water tank and pumped in some fresh water. And when she had drunk her fill and snorted water all about the place, he tied the big animal off in the shade of the spreading live oak under which I had built a rail and a swing seat for Annie and me. It was a five-mile ride from Peaceful, the county seat, and it was a hot day and he looked done in.

I first met Gus Street, Blackwater's long time county sheriff, ten or so years after the war soon after I quit New Orleans. I was looking for a small spread in which to sink some loose cash for a future I did not, in reality, expect to see. Peaceful, the county seat, sounded promising and although there was paper on me in Montana, Harry Beaudine kept such trivialities clear of me in Wyoming, probably on account of him being the US Marshal thereabouts. I was looking over the property when Street happened by and, much to my chagrin, he recognized me right off from a Montana warrant, but it seems he also knew Harry Beaudine and made it clear from the get go that he had no interest in me whatsoever apart from the likelihood of me being his neighbour. He owned the adjacent property and ran a few cows and a small *remuda* of saddle-broke horses he hired to the local ranchers come the spring roundup.

'You as good with that six as they say

you are, Mr Santana?' he had asked me that first meeting.

'Probably not,' I had replied.

He fished a tin can out of the brush, looked at me and tossed it high in the air. Just like a hound dog reacting to a thrown stick, I pulled and fired three fast rounds, bouncing the can in the air. When it had settled, he retrieved it, examined it and said with a broad smile, 'Not so hot, you missed one.'

I remember clearly returning his grin. 'I'm more of the glass is half-full kind of man, Sheriff, and would prefer to say I hit it twice.'

He nodded and tossed the can back into the brush as I pulled again and fired, the round taking the can when it was only inches from his fingers. He yelled and swore as he leaped backwards, tripped, sat down on his ample backside and snorted, 'Goddamn that was fancy! You damned near took my fingers off!'

'There you go again,' I said, 'always with the negativity, always the pessimist.'

And I burst out laughing. We both did. That kind of settled it for me. I bought the property, called it Wildcat and we have been friends ever since. On occasion I even helped him out as a part-time deputy.

'What is the pleasure of this visit, Gus?' The elderly man wore a dusty brown town suit. I guessed it was too hot for him to wear the grey duster tied behind his saddle. He was, I reckoned, in his mid-sixties, tall but a little bent now with either age or worry. I was not sure of which, but it was election year so I put it down to the latter. His smile was still broad, though, and split his darkly-tanned face wide when he exposed it, which was, I had noticed, not so often of late. He had a drooping moustache, and dark deep-set eyes in a long face. The visible hair at his temples peeping out from beneath his broad, flat-brimmed, black, high-crowned Stetson hat was grey. He settled on the swing seat and I propped myself against the hitching rail and waited.

'Got a Montana wolver in town yesterday afternoon, name of Henry Briggs, says you took a shot at him, stole his rifle and mule and ran him off up by Willard's Rocks, which he claims to be open range. Now we both know that it isn't so, but the rifle and the mule — what was that about?'

I laughed. 'I loosed his mule, but I guess it was too smart to go home. As for the rifle, I kept that as payment for killing that big cat I like feeding up there.'

'That old cougar you call Spirit of the West? That was the cat? He did that?'

'He did that, yes.'

'You still have the rifle?'

'Yes and no. By that I mean I still have, but not here. It's already on its way to a friend in Cheyenne, to cut down to a carbine — easier to handle and carry on a horse. I know a US marshal down there one time, he has one like that, had it customized. Shortened the barrel by three inches of a standard model 1874, an Old Reliable they call it. Fires a long .45 calibre round. He fitted double extractors to pull out those hot cases. Three inches longer than your usual saddle carbine and you wouldn't want to be within a mile of it. Wally Dade, you may know him. They call him Goddamned Wally Dade on account he says that word frequently. One time he had such a weapon and I always wanted one of those Sharps and that damned wolver's is a real beauty.'

'Best you keep it then, but watch out for Briggs and his two companions. They are a mean trio and, although not too popular around here, they do keep the wolves and the cougars down for those ranchers that do not share your love of wild critters like wolves and cats. Least ways, not the way you do.'

'Sadly, they are getting to be few and far between in this neck of the woods.'

'That's because your neighbours hire thugs like Briggs and his ilk to kill them.'

'Not on my land they don't. You

know it is posted against hunting. You set that up for me as I recall.'

'Yes, I did, but that doesn't mean I always agree with you, Lucas.' He gave me that weary lawman look. 'Who the hell is the Peaceful River Kid?'

'Never heard of that *hombre*,' I said.

He gave me that you go to hell, you lying sonofabitch look, smiled and said, 'Anyhow, they have moved on now but they will be back this way in a couple of months and will not have forgotten you. Hate is a heavy rock to carry and that *hombre* looks pretty strong. It could mean trouble for you further down the line, but I'll keep an eye on things in town.' He looked at me long and hard, sniffed the air, and said, 'Stew, I do believe I can smell a sonofa-gun stew coming on.'

'That's right, Gus, a bit of everything.'

'A fine cook, that lady of yours. Let's wash up and get to it. Oh and by the way, you got a telegraph from Cheyenne, Harry Beaudine.' He pulled a creased sheet of thin paper from his coat pocket and handed it to me and watched carefully as I read it. 'Guess you will be leaving us again for a while. The job must pay well for you to leave this little part of Heaven.'

I wasn't too thrilled about leaving Annie and Wildcat so soon after my previous assignment, but the money would help keep the ranch running until I had built up enough stock to sell and horses to trade. And besides, I was tired of digging fence holes. Maybe I could earn a little extra dinero to sweeten the pot this time around and when I returned, hire someone to dig the damned things while I loafed around. There was no explanation in the note, just instructions of where to go. Beaudine was careful like that when hiring me, trusting nothing to paper in case it back-fired on his department. He would leave me staked out in the sun if necessary to save his precious department, but on the other hand he would see to it that backup, should I need it, would not be far away. And if I made an extra dollar along the way, he would turn a blind eye to that. South West Texas, a long haul by rail and he must need me real bad. Intriguing.

2

A Town Called Dry Water

So, that's it about me, and more to the point why was I riding down the dusty Main Street of Dry Water, South Texas, on a newly-acquired sweet-tempered bay Morgan in the middle of a hot August afternoon when any sane man would be sitting in the shade, sleeping or fishing for crappies in the cotton-wood shade of the nearby Dry Water Creek. The creek from which the town took its name was an anomaly; no one as far as I ever heard tell could say where the name came from. The creek is cold mountain water fed and had never run dry. Even then, on a hot day I could see dark clouds over the distant Sierras and smell the sweet perfume of rain on the distant wind. I knew that rain would not reach Dry Water Creek,

29

but its falling would feed the distant gullies and rush on down to the valley and refill the creek with fresh water to replace that stolen from it by the midday sun.

That much I had learned about the town before riding its Main Street. It pays a man in my profession to be very aware of his surroundings, surroundings that often shape the people he is likely to encounter therein. The answer to the why I was there is, I did not know. In the pocket of my much-washed and sun-bleached Levi's was a letter from US Marshal Harry Beaudine of Cheyenne telling me to be there and that I would be contacted by someone from the San Antonio Pinkerton office and that, should I take the job, I would be paid at the usual rate of ten dollars a day, considerably more than a deputy US marshal earns, and if said job went belly-up I would be disowned by the Service. That's another 'usual' I had come to accept.

★ ★ ★

Dry Water, a small Texas town, was probably booming when beef was big, but now not so much. The war was a long time passing and folk were not so hungry for meat, the small ranches mostly taken over, swallowed up by corporations, bigger companies run by men from the east, faceless men with unfamiliar names, names that appeared on foreclosure notices or end-of-the-line notices for free-wheeling cowboys. Texas was changing and not necessarily for the better, but that was not my worry though. Texas would be just another job.

The expected store fronts were mostly shabby and in need of some paint — a barber's pole, an assay office, general store, bank, timber yard and livery stable, two hotels, a diner, a saloon, billiards room, Overland Stage and post office. A doctor's shingle hung lop-sided from a rusting chain handily next door to an undertaker's establishment. The Wayside Tavern was across the street from an adobe cantina and a brick-built sheriff's office. The latter run, I guessed, by a deputy as it was thirty miles from the county seat of Marlborough. It was a backwater and probably of little interest to anyone other than the people who lived, worked and likely died there. Surprisingly there was a small newspaper office with a shingle that read *The Dry Water Bugle*. I reined in the bay in front of the livery and was greeted by a weary-looking boy, his eyes lighting up at the pretty Morgan. I gave him two bits and instructions on what the pony needed, returned his smile and, carrying my saddle-bags and warbag on my shoulder and Winchester rifle at the trail, I crossed Main Street and entered the larger of the two hotels, the Cattlemen's, and registered under the name of Louis Bassett of Wichita. The chubby disinterested-looking desk clerk gave me a key attached to a large numbered chunk of wood, and I checked into my room.

After a quick wash to remove some of the day's dust, I headed for the larger of the two saloons, overcome with a thirst for a cold beer and a sudden hunger for a hard-boiled egg or two. A large, mean-looking black mongrel dog stirred as I passed the general store come millinery, walked a step or two toward me, sniffed the air, decided a close look at my boot was worth the effort, allowed me to ruffle its long neck hair and settled back down closing one eye and keeping the other on my passing. From the corner of my eye, I saw the drawn window curtain of the millinery move and guessed that maybe the town dog wasn't the only soul in Dry Water taking an interest in me.

The interior of the Wayside Tavern was dark and smelled of stale smoke and fresh sawdust. It took a long moment for my eyes to adjust back down after the brightness of the outside midday sun. I stood just inside of the batwing doors, allowing my vision to compensate for the lack of light. In my line of work it is a given that you did not walk into a public place without having some idea as to what or who was already in there. In this case, there was very little and, apart from two elderly men in drab town suits, their jackets hanging on the backs of their chairs, their unyielding concentration focused on the dominoes in front of them, the place was empty of customers. The pair took less interest in me than had the dog. The barkeep in his fresh white apron looked up from the newspaper he was reading and waited as I approached the bar, took an egg from the jar and sprinkled my palm with salt from the shaker and bit off the end.

'You want a drink to go with that egg, mister?'

I nodded.

'A cold beer would be good.'

I watched as he fed the glass from the tap. It had a big head on it.

'Two bits.'

I gave him a quarter, which he dropped into the cash drawer, closed it and returned to his paper without giving me a second look. A bartender, a dog, two old barflies and a moving curtain;

no one seemed much interested in me. I am used to attracting a little more attention than that; my tooled black leather gunbelt, with the cross-draw belly rig with the ivory handled grips of the .44-40 Colt protruding from the matching black leather holster, hand-tooled and sewn in El Paso, usually received more than a passing interest.

'Quiet town,' I said to no one in particular.

The barkeep, a stocky, florid-faced elderly man with a waxed moustache matching the colour of his red, greased back hair, looked up from his paper, held my gaze for a moment and returned to his reading, muttering. 'That's the way we like it.'

I finished the beer and asked for another. 'Can I buy you one?' I said. 'I hate drinking alone.'

Almost a smile. 'Sure enough.'

He tapped out two more beers and this time wiped the large heads off with a wooden spatula before topping them up and passing one to me. I dropped two quarters onto the bar and he scooped them up.

'Come far?'

'Far enough in this heat,' I said, wiping my moustache of the remaining froth. 'You got the makings? I'm out.'

He reached under the bar and tossed me a half-full sack of Bull Durham. 'Help yourself.'

I nodded my thanks, stripped a Rizla, filled it with dusty tobacco, pulled the tab tight with my teeth and passed it back to him. It was a fair enough quirly and I fired it with one of the blue top matches nestling in the hollow of a large brick.

'You have a name?' I asked.

'Red,' he said. 'Red is short for Redmond, not because of the colour of my hair. Red O'Bannion.' There was that gentle touch of the Irish in his deep voice and I wondered if he could sing.

He did not ask me my name, seemingly more interested suddenly in the Colt lying across my left hip. I gave it to him anyway. 'Muddy John Rivers.

My father had a great sense of humour.'

The lie came easy; it was a name and a line I had used often enough before. I wasn't certain whether there were any outstanding warrants on me in Marlborough County, but I couldn't be sure and erred to caution.

'They call you Mud?'

It was a genuine question.

'Not too many people call me that, Red, mostly they call me Rivers.'

'No offence meant, mister . . . '

'And none taken, Red,' I assured him with my winning smile.

He leaned forward, his elbows propped on the bar top. 'Not so quiet here usually but the cattle and the drovers all headed north late summer after the roundup and won't be back for a while, spending all of their money in the big towns at end of track and then come back here broke to loaf in my saloon. The local cowhands and ranchers don't spend too much of anything these days, time or money. Can be lively on a Saturday night, though, when Danny Doyle's men are in town.'

'You own this saloon?' I was genuinely surprised.

'Tavern, I call it a tavern. It has a little bit more class to it and it separates it from the Bullhorn Cantina and its forty-rod rotgut across the street.'

'And Danny Doyle?' I asked.

'He owns a lot of the countryside around here.'

I thought about that. There was a scraping of chairs behind me and I watched in the mirror as the two old men climbed wearily to their feet and nodded to the tavern owner as they shuffled across the freshly saw-dusted plank floor. I wondered how long they had made a couple of beers last that day. He must have read my mind.

'Three hours clicking those damned dominoes and their teeth, spent a dollar between them. Sometimes I wonder why I bother this time of the year, late summer and fall is always quiet and winter even quieter.'

I nodded sympathetically and asked, 'Where is the best place to get a meal this time of the day?'

'Try the Green Frog up by Doyle's Bank and Loan Company. Molly will fix you up something whatever the time of day. Good grub there as well.'

I thanked him, settled my hat a little lower over my eyes and walked out into the bright sunshine and headed for the diner, pausing on the way to buy some tobacco from the general store. I noted, amused, the sign over the diner's wide door showed the painting of a green frog and the words *Prop: Redmond O'Bannion*. I wondered what else he owned. Whatever, he was right about the food, thick rashers of bacon, two eggs and hot beans, mostly grease-free and hot. The coffee I washed it all down with wasn't half bad, considering the muck I had to drink along the trail since leaving the train at San Antonio. Molly was a rotund, mature, good-natured Irishwoman and I guessed either the wife or kin of the tavern owner. I paid her and complimented her, saying I would be returning for breakfast. She gave me a broad smile and told me I would be most welcome.

I bought a bottle of whiskey in the general store, which I discovered was also owned by O'Bannion, and ordered a bath out back of the hotel. I soaked an hour, put on some fresh clothes, sent the dirty ones to the Chinese laundry also out back of the hotel, and settled down on the hard bed. Arms folded behind my head, I studied the cracked water-stained ceiling wondering, among other things, how long it would be before US Marshal Harry Beaudine's man made contact. Not too long I hoped.

3

The Lady, the Dog and the Deputy

I stayed in my room that evening, sipped on my bottle and smoked from the fresh sack of tobacco. I am not a great smoker, but now and then, when in reflective mood, it is useful to look at the world, the past especially, through the haze of tobacco smoke. It distorts and sometimes, with the aid of the whiskey, helps to make events to come and those gone by a little more bearable. I am what I have become, a gun for hire, a sometime bounty hunter, sometime lawman and, according to the wanted fliers in several states and counties, a sometime outlaw. I have never brought a man down from cover and never, within sensible reason, pulled first. I have worked for Allan Pinkerton's detective agency and the

US Marshal's Service, but always with the latter in a hired capacity, never from behind a badge. I would, I know, find the constraints untenable.

The first man I ever killed face-to-face was at Gettysburg and little more than a boy, while I was already a veteran at eighteen. Gettysburg. A misty morning the day before the battle, I was walking through the grey, shrouded woods that would soon be torn apart by cannon fire when I came face to face with a young man in Union Blue. He was a lieutenant of cavalry and he had a Remington revolver in one hand and large dead jack rabbit in the other. When the shock of the encounter had passed, he raised the gun, cocked it and fired. The round took the epaulet from the right shoulder of my grey tunic. My Colt was in its holster, flap down. I cleared the flap and pulled fast just as he loosed a second round which chewed the bark off a tree near to my ear. As he cocked it for a third round, I fired my pistol straight-armed like a duellist, the round taking him in the chest, throwing him back against a live oak. His dying body slid down the tree's trunk, only halting when his spurred boot heels struck a root, bending his knees up under his chin. Devastated, I had rushed to his side, cradled his head and wiped the blood from his lips, much as I had with Darryl Jones. He looked up at me, showing no pain or anger and said simply, 'Eat the rabbit, please eat the rabbit.' Then he coughed and died. 'Eat the rabbit.' I often hear those three words, especially on nights like this in a cheap hotel room or under the stars on some forgotten trail, like that soldier alone and perhaps a little lost.

*   *   *

Molly was cheerful at breakfast and I bumped into O'Bannion just as he was leaving. He smiled and said, 'Great cook, terrible wife.' Her smile told me that was not so, just marriage banter, something I missed when away from Wyoming.

I checked in on the Morgan mare and was pleased to see her coat was gleaming, her stall clean with fresh hay a-plenty. I thanked the boy and gave him another two bits and told him I would be around for several days and would settle with the livery owner when I left as was the custom. I bought a pack of five stogies from the general store and settled on the porch in front of the Wayside Tavern with the chair rocked back and one foot on the veranda rail. No sooner had I made myself comfortable than the town dog wandered over, looked me over and settled down beside the chair and promptly went to sleep.

'He likes you,' she said. 'More than I can say for most folk. They usually give him their boot, but I watched, you yesterday and you did not.'

Her voice was soft, almost husky, a hint of an accent. She was around forty-five years old, slim without being thin, attractive of face in a strong-featured masculine kind of way. She had auburn hair and wore a loose-fitting flower-patterned dress, the print flowers mostly blood red. She smelled perfumed and sweet. I slammed the front legs of the chair down and got to my feet, removing my hat and momentarily lost for words, guessing hers was the hand behind the moving millinery curtain on the previous day.

'His name is Bart, Black Bart after the poet stagecoach robber, and he does not belong to anyone. He likes you — you are not an outlaw or a poet, are you?' She smiled a distant, wistful kind of smile.

'No, I am not an outlaw or a poet. Do I look like either?'

'Not in that hat, I guess. But what do outlaws and poets look like, I wouldn't know?'

'My name is John Moon,' I said, holding out my hand. She took it, a puzzled look on her face.

'I heard you were called Muddy

Rivers,' she said.

'I cannot think where you heard that,' I said.

She shook her head.

'Kathleen Riley,' she said, holding my hand for a long moment before releasing it, her fair-skinned face slightly flushed.

'Is everyone in this town Irish?' I said.

'No, not everyone,' she said, 'just most of us.'

'What makes you think I am a *desperado*?' I asked.

'Small town, people observe, talk, come to conclusions, often wrong ones, but it passes a quiet afternoon.'

'And what have the good people of Dry Water observed?' I asked, smiling at her, standing there with Black Bart at my feet and my hat in my hand.

'You wear your gun outside your pants. Not too many do that unless they are cowhands coming in from the range for a quick drink before going home.'

'I noticed that.'

'Sheriff Hadley frowns on such things.'

'You mean Deputy Sheriff Hadley,

don't you?' I said.

'I stand corrected, Mr Moon. Good day to you, sir.' She began to move away and I touched her arm briefly and she paused.

'You run the millinery, am I right?'

'I also run the local newspaper, the *Bugle*. Are you going to allow me to interview you?'

'I doubt anyone in this town would find that of any interest.'

She smiled a lovely white-toothed smile. 'You would be surprised how much interest there is in you already, sir. We do not get many strangers passing through here this time of the year.'

I watched her walk away, wishing she had lingered a little longer. Bart raised his head, looked at me and then at Kathleen Riley's slim back, closed his eyes and went back to sleep.

★　★　★

The next interruption to my siesta was not so pleasurable. I had just dozed off, my foot back on the rail, when Bart growled, a low deep-throated growl. I looked up and saw a big figure dressed in black moving along the rutted street toward me. I tipped my hat back. It was a tall, bulky man, his back to the sun. I waited, telling the dog to be still; for some reason it obeyed me. The man stopped a few feet from me, dark-faced with long hair and a drooping moustache; either he thought it attractive or he wanted to be Earp or Bill Hickok, who had both favoured such an appearance at one time or another. A white scar ran from his ear to his lower lip. I wondered if that was why he favoured a moustache. He stared down at the black dog, his coat dropping open revealing a five-pointed fancy star on his vest and the side view of a tan shoulder holster under his left arm.

'I would walk around him, Deputy, were I you. He is in one bad mood. I put it down to the heat — what do you think?'

He switched his gaze from the dog to

me. 'One of these days I'll put a round through his dark hide.' He was softly spoken, his hoarse voice grating.

'Not on my watch I hope, Deputy Hadley.' I kept my tone light, unthreatening.

'Sheriff Hadley to you, mister whatever you name is.' His voice had hardened.

'No, sir,' I said, 'Sheriff Dave Murdock is over at the county seat in Marlborough. You are a deputy, best learn to live with it.'

'You know Murdock?'

'We are acquainted,' I lied.

'I don't like to see a man wearing a sidearm in my town.'

'Not your town and not your rules, no Dry Water town ordinance forbidding a man wearing his piece inside or outside of his pants, I looked that up.' Another lie. 'This is Texas, after all.'

'Listen, Bassett or Moon or Rivers or whatever the hell it is, I don't like the folk of my town being made fools of by some Yankee slick. Best you get your business, whatever that is, done and get a lot of gone between you and me.'

'Some folk call me the Peaceful River Kid,' I said, broadening my winning smile. 'Are you running me out of Dodge, Deputy Hadley?'

'Call it any way you like, just do it.'

He turned on his heel and stomped off along the covered boardwalk, his dark boots raising little wisps of dust with every step.

I had heard it all before and he was right in some respects. The need to wear a gun was long gone and, other than cowboys in from the range or young men out to impress young women, it was mostly a peace officer would be the only man walking the street with a gun on his hip. Many towns in the west had city or town ordinances against the wearing of side arms whilst within the town limits, and I usually respect those rules, but Hadley rubbed me up the wrong way. Changing times and old habits die hard.

'You sure pissed off our deputy, Mr Bassett, Moon or Rivers. He doesn't take kindly to folk calling him deputy.' It was O'Bannion, talking over the closed batwing doors. 'You coming in for a beer or are you going to sit there and sweat.'

'You got one for the dog?'

'Sure, why not — you're both crazy.'

It turned out O'Bannion was, like most bartenders, a fountain of knowledge, a generally good-natured man who liked to talk over a cold beer and had no trouble at all with made-up names. And if he wondered just why they were made up, I guessed he had learned a long time ago not to ask.

4

The History Lesson

The Tavern was empty apart from O'Bannion and he looked to me in need of a drinking companion so, followed by the mutt, I walked into the welcoming shade, and O'Bannion had two headless beers on the bar top when I was still two steps away. Seeing the dog, he half-filled a shallow basin and set that beside the beers, I tossed a fifty cent piece on the polished bar top and placed the dish down beside my boot. Bart lapped it up, belched and wandered off to a dark corner from which his one open eye gave him a good clear dog's eye view of the room.

The Tavern's owner was in a talkative mood and Pinkerton had once advised me on the merits of finding a willing source and milking it for all it was worth and to worry about the merits of the gained information at a later date. Being a Scotsman of few words, Pinkerton's advice was short and succinct; as I recall, to 'keep your mouth shut and listen.' So, that is exactly what I did as the big man refilled our glasses from time to time and imparted the history of Dry Water. In the telling of his story, O'Bannion made himself out to be the good guy and I had no idea as to the truth of it, but I listened and drank while the big Irishman talked and drank, his eyes often misting over as he remembered a faraway place. A long-gone home in distant County Kerry far from the dust and the dry heat of South Texas.

'It rains a great deal in Ireland and the grass grows fine. The cows give the sweetest of creamy milk and the potatoes kept the farmers fed. Seemed like a paradise and nothing could go wrong. You ever lived in place like that, Rivers?'

I thought of Wyoming, clear running water, and a warm breeze. 'Sure enough,

I've got such a spread like that in Wyoming.'

'That's a long ways away. What the hell are you doing in this place, West Texas? One of these days will come along a strong Norther and it will all blow away.'

'Just passing through, Red. I do not aim to stay here.'

'Don't stay too long, son. Things can change very quickly. It did for us.'

'How come?' I asked.

'You ever heard of the potato famine?'

'No,' I lied. Like I said, I am very well-read.

'In 1845 a blight hit the crops and suddenly that paradise became a dying Hell. I stayed for as long as I could, helped out where I was able, but I could see no end to it.' He sipped his beer, topped up our glasses and stared off into space, his thoughts far from Dry Water, West Texas. 'They say over a million people died because of it. Can you imagine that number of people dying because a god-damned spud crop failed?'

'Were you a farmer?' I asked in the long silence that followed the question to which I had no answer.

'Heavens no! As here, I was into business, owned several general stores mostly selling to the farmers, and when they went broke or quit so did I.' He smiled sadly, 'Strange how we all interlock, how one life depends upon another.'

'You quit?'

'No point in staying; the countryside was dying and it was too painful to watch. Near the end, in 1850, I could see the whole country was going down the crapper and I had no intention of going with it. I decided to quit the old country and emigrate to greener pastures far across the Atlantic Ocean. I have never regretted that move, but the old country still rattles my old bones now and then.'

'That it, you just packed a bag and left?'

'Nothing else to do.'

'You have a family?'

'No, thank the good Lord. I just grabbed my savings and suitcase, packed up what I could carry and headed for the docks. Before leaving I threw open the stores, hung signs telling folk to help themselves to what little I had left to offer. Me and Danny Doyle, not birds of a feather exactly, but he was an amiable enough travelling companion.'

The two old men stomped into the bar, walked around Bart and took up their usual seats, rattling the dominoes and signalling with a wave to O'Bannion for beer. The big man sighed and muttered something under his breath about big spenders. He served them, refilled our glasses at the same time, and waved away my offer to pay for them.

'On the house. Where was I?'

'Doyle,' I said.

'Ah yes, Danny Doyle. Now there's a man to walk around should you run into him during your stay, Mr Muddy Rivers.' He paused, smiling. 'That's never your real name, is it?'

It wasn't really a question, so I did not treat it as one.

'Was Doyle also a store keeper?' I asked.

'No, far too ambitious. Doyle was a money lender and capitalized on the hardships suffered by those less fortunate. He foreclosed on the broken farmers, resold the land at a profit to the land-hungry and often absent English, the large estate owners, pocketed the profit and joined me on the first available ship out of harbour. He had two suitcases and a larger poke than I.' He smiled ruefully, adding, 'A much larger poke. Why are you so interested in this town anyway?'

'Nosey, I guess. I am a listener. I listen a lot and knowing about the people in a strange town like this helps pass a long day.'

'You really passing through or hanging around to meet someone?'

'Who knows,' I said. 'Interesting people cross my path all the time.'

'You on the dodge? Is there paper on you somewhere?'

'Hey, Red,' I said very quietly, 'if I told you that I would have to shoot you down.'

He stared at me for a long moment and then burst out laughing. And I joined him.

'Fair enough, I guess. Shoot me in my own place? I don't believe so, but I know sure enough when I am being told to mind my own business.'

★   ★   ★

O'Bannion rambled on and I got the idea that he painted Danny Doyle pretty dark compared to his own role in the growth of Dry Water and, although the two men were only briefly acquainted through business, they soon found that they fitted well together on the crowded confines of the ship. Better than mingling with the poor and often sickly farming families in steerage. It seemed that every day the ship paused, sails lowered, to bury the dead in a coal black, unfeeling sea. The two men shared one of the few cabins and ate often at the captain's table, making the best of a bad situation. On reaching what many on board that stinking troubled ship considered to be the Promised Land, they headed for San Antonio, got lost and wound up in the South Texas one-horse town named Dry Water Creek.

According to Red O'Bannion, initially neither man prospered, but with the advent of the Civil War in 1861 both men came into their own. O'Bannion bought up the empty lots in the town and built a store, a saloon, a new hotel, a restaurant and even a small freight and haulage line, and within those buildings created a thriving business empire as a hungry war devoured whatever he had to offer. He also married a fellow immigrant, an attractive young Irishwoman who had, along with others, also discovered Dry Water Creek.

Doyle, on the other hand, purchased much of the surrounding countryside and settled his Purgatory ranch on the best of the land. There he raised cattle or stole them from below the borderline and sold them at an enormous profit to the Confederacy, whilst O'Bannion did the same with smuggled goods from Mexico. Those four years, that were for the pair the best of times and for the rest of America the worst of times, did not last long; but while they did, both men grew in stature and reputation. O'Bannion the philanthropist and much-loved mayor of the township and Doyle the bullying landowner and banker who would not tolerate free-grazers or settlers, even though much of the land surrounding his property was open range and under federal jurisdiction.

O'Bannion described his one-time travelling companion as a man of bad temper, a big man, fat, red-faced and who usually had an entourage of gunmen with him, the worst of whom was his trusted confidant and bodyguard, Elmore Cream. Cream was a man of mixed race, possibly Comanche but more likely the offspring of a Yaqui. He was, O'Bannion said, every inch a gunfighter and general heavy. He usually rode in concert with half a dozen men dressed in long black dusters, O'Bannion said they scared the 'living bejesus' out of all who happened to cross Doyle's crooked path. Doyle himself was not beyond using his cane, which housed within its polished wood frame the long metal barrel of a four-ten shotgun, with which he had, to O'Bannion's certain knowledge, killed at least two men and crippled another. He was an arrogant man who, without consultation, changed the name of the township by dropping the word Creek, which he considered demeaning.

As the war drew to its inevitable conclusion and Robert E. Lee surrendered at Appomattox Court House, so the trade and the money dried up. O'Bannion's enterprises were still needed, although much reduced — men still required saloons and haircuts, and drummers still needed hotel rooms. Different though for Doyle, and when the military's need for cattle in quantity dwindled, so too did his income evaporate. At one time, to hear O'Bannion tell it, the rancher was near broke and only survived due to the intervention of an eastern philanthropist, a painter with some romantic notions of the Old West, whom he made his partner. A doomed and brief partnership as it turned out to be, when the artist was found bloated, black and very dead in a gully, a suspected victim of a diamondback, so common in the rocky countryside. On his easel was an unfinished painting of a countryside much greener than it actually was.

'I'm not saying Doyle had anything to do with the man's dying out there, but then again I am not saying he did not. Trouble is with men like Danny Doyle, they are hard to read. How far would he go, I do not know and would hate to find out.'

'I think I would very much like to meet this Danny Doyle sometime,' I said, finishing my fifth beer and waving away a refill.

'Stick around long enough and that is inevitable. He has already shown more than a little curiosity regarding your presence in Dry Water. Hadley was enquiring about you and he is a conduit direct to friend Doyle. You will need to watch your step there, son.'

5

The Pinkerton Woman

And that was it really, although I believe O'Bannion would have said a lot more had not the place suddenly become alive as the late afternoon and early evening drinkers dropped by for a wet before going home to supper or, as I had intended, drift along to the Green Frog for mine. My intention had been just that, an early night and an early start for me and the Morgan to survey the surrounding countryside, just in case I would ever need a quick way out or a place to hide. A man can never be too careful and a place to run is often a necessity for survival. My plans changed somewhat when I stepped outside and, followed by Bart, crossed the street to where Kathleen Riley was waving to me.

'You spend a great deal of your time in saloons, Mr. Whateveryournameis.'

I touched the brim of my hat. 'Sorry, Miss Riley, I did not know you were waiting on me.'

'Kathleen, please, and I wasn't exactly waiting, but I was hoping to see you today.'

'*Bugle* business or millinery?' I asked.

'*Bugle*, I think. I don't have anything in your size. Would you like to come in for coffee?' She looked down at Bart and then back at me. 'Is he with you or are you with him?'

'We seem to have become a bit of a package and I have no idea as to the why of it, but animals, old ladies and children take a liking to me. Is he welcome? Probably better house-trained than me.'

She smiled her wide smile and pushed open the door. Bart followed her and I followed him.

The store was roughly divided in two. One half, the larger of the areas, was the general store with its ubiquitous black pot-bellied stove and cracker barrel surrounded by several barroom chairs. General everyday supplies were shelved and a glass case of handguns served as part of the counter, backed up by a half empty rack of chained long guns. The other half was taken up with a long counter littered with bolts of colourful material. The coffee pot on top of the stove was steaming.

I sat down on one of the chairs and watched as she set down a bowl of water for the dog before filling two tin mugs with dark coffee. 'Would you like a shot, Lucas?' she asked innocently.

I did not react or in any way show my surprise at her use of my name. After years behind playing cards over countless poker tables, I have developed an unreadable face and even the deal coming from such an apparently innocent and pretty mouth did not throw me.

'If you will join me, Kathleen, I could use one. O'Bannion's beer is fine, but it does not exactly hit the spot.'

'I would not let you drink alone.' She produced a bottle from behind the counter and poured two generous shots into our steaming mugs. 'O'Bannion's best imported Irish.'

'Do you mind if I smoke?' I asked.

'Not at all, please do and pass the makings to me when you are done.'

'Ladies first,' I said. I tossed her the new sack of Durham and watched as she rolled an exquisitely neat quirly and fired it with a blue top match, and took a gentle pull of smoke.

She watched in an amused silence as I rolled a far less neat cigarette and fired it, drawing manfully deep and slowly expelling the hot smoke.

I let the silence between us last until the coffee was drunk and a refill declined, and asked, 'And why exactly am I here?'

'You don't know?'

She reached into her small black purse, peeled back a strip of lining, removed an engraved card and passed it to me. 'Allan said you were a man of many facets, but neglected to mention that you were also a man of many names. I like Lucas Santana better than the others and certainly better than the Peaceful River Kid. Where exactly is the Peaceful River anyway?'

'Wyoming,' I said. 'Pretty country, a little windy at times, but more colourful than Texas.'

I took the card but did not look at it. I had seen many just like it before, even carried one myself from time to time. 'How long has Pinkerton been employing women agents?' I asked, handing her back the card.

'Before the war. I believe the first was in 1856, Kate Warne, and now we are no longer a rarity and we have our own department. Do you object, Mr Santana?'

'I did not know that and no, I have no objections. Just so long as you don't put me out of a job.'

'Not likely. We just sit around listening, watching, noting and then pass it on to you rough-and-tumble, pistol-packing agents who get the job finished. For instance, Allan set up the *Bugle* for just such a purpose. I can dig around, ask a lot of fool questions, but nobody really takes much notice of me other than in the hope of seeing their name in print for just about any reason short of murder.' She chuckled and it sounded like the clear water rushing over the rocks at the base of my small Wyoming mountain stream, where the big cat used to drink.

'I'm not exactly an agent,' I said.

'I know. You prefer to go freelance, it's better pay. But Allan told me to treat you as if you were one of us. Also, you are a friend of US Marshal Harry Beaudine, and we all respect that man.'

'Is Harry involved in this deal?'

'It's his call, all of the way, a federal investigation. He has hired Pinkerton and Allan has sub-contracted to you. And I will be so happy to see the back of Dry Water now that you are here and I can get back to my lover in San Antonio.'

'Lucky man. Does he know what

your daytime job is?'

She ignored that question and waited for another and I obliged, feeling a little foolish. 'Is it Federal?'

'Very Federal, US Treasury Federal.'

'War loot?'

'Yes.'

'Gold or silver?'

'Gold.'

'How much?'

'No one seems absolutely sure about that.' She shrugged, rocked her shoulders, shook her head and, smiling, said, 'Maybe three quarters of a million in coin and bullion.'

'I'm hungry,' I said. 'Happy to play guessing games, but would be happier if you told me and then I could buy you supper and we could be friends and I could tell you about the Peaceful River and my Teton Sioux wife, a lady I would like to get back to just as much as I guess you would be to your man in San Antonio.'

'I'm sorry to tease, but you are an easy mark for a hazing. Is it Lucas or do you prefer Luke?'

'Either is good, but Lucas has a more mature ring to it.'

'At the end of the war, a large shipment of gold in the form of 20-dollar double eagle gold pieces, no one seems sure of the exact amount, was hijacked somewhere around here. The gold was on its way to Dallas, accompanied by a small unit of federal troops, ten in number counting their commanding officer. Both they and the gold vanished.' She paused and refilled her cup. I declined.

'When was this?' I asked.

'Just after the peace. It was money for the various garrisons assigned hereabouts to see that order was kept and that no advantage was taken of us, the vanquished.' There was a bitterness in her words. 'We were never vanquished. Texas was always Texas and the men who chose to fight fought and died for Texas and not for the Confederacy.'

'You lost someone in the war?'

'My husband, Bradley, Hood's Texas

Brigade. He fell at Nashville — what a waste.'

I let the silence settle around us. I am of the opinion that the bereaved need to talk and the living need to listen and that any words of comfort offered are meaningless.

She smiled a sad smile. 'It was a long time ago, but sometimes it seems like only yesterday.'

'Yes, it does, Kathleen. I was with Hood, but not at Nashville. Strange man in many ways, but he attracted a very loyal following.'

'You were also Infantry?'

'No, a mounted scout patrol. We rode ahead of the main infantry force much as the Yankees did and sadly, like the Yankees, we didn't always get back.'

'Small world, isn't it just.'

'Seems to get smaller every day.'

'I am so pleased you told me that. Brad seems so long ago and far away now.'

'I will take that drink if it's still on offer,' I said quietly.

She carefully topped up my mug and, looking me straight in the eye, said, 'One more thing, Lucas.' She was suddenly a Pinkerton agent again and in the moment, a weary trip back from a painful past. 'I was told to give you this.' She walked across the room and unlocked a cupboard, returning with a small package.

I opened it and shook out a leather badge holder and identity card. The badge was for a deputy US Marshal and the card was unallocated but issued clearly by the State Department and bore the signature of the US Attorney General. I shook my head and handed it back to her but she did not take it.

'Harry Beaudine was most emphatic about this. You have to take it. You need not wear it, but we are travelling in a grey area down here and his influence or that of Allan Pinkerton may not stretch this far south of San Antonio.'

I looked down at the nickel-plated badge and then up at her. 'I don't like them. You wear it over your heart, a sure-fire target, yet it will not stop a bullet, more likely a round from a forty-five will drive the damned thing deep into your body. A badge is bad news.'

'Please take it.'

'Will it make you happy?'

'Yes, very.'

I put the wallet into my inside jacket pocket. 'For you, then.'

Kathleen Riley poured another two shots into our tin cups, we clicked them together in a silent toast to the living and the dead, and we drained the bottle dry.

★   ★   ★

Over supper in a quiet corner of the Green Frog, Kathleen told me that she had been in Dry Water for six months listening and learning. The *Bugle*, set up by Pinkerton as a cover and welcomed by most of the township, gave her the opportunity to pry and ask questions where an ordinary citizen would not.

The Frog was pretty much deserted and Molly had gone home by the time we arrived and Kathleen was amused at my insistence on sitting with my back to the wall. 'It's an old habit,' I told her. 'I am not being overly dramatic, but it pays to be careful. Remember, Bill Hickock wasn't the first lawman to get it in the back. Morgan Earp went down and Bucky Thorenson was crippled.'

'I remember Bucky. He was a Pinkerton man through and through,' she said.

'I never met him,' I said. 'But it's a habit newspapermen might want to pick up,' I added, only half-jokingly. It could be a dangerous profession where a great deal of money might hang on the word of a news report.

'If we both sat with our backs to the wall it would look a little strange.' Again that chuckle. 'On the whole, reporters are just naturally nosy and few people believe what we write in any case, so it is an ideal front.'

'Why Dry Water, though?'

'Dry Water was chosen because of the death of a Mexican, a suspected bandit. His body was found by a Texas Ranger face down in a small run-off from Dry Water Creek, which itself is a run-off from the Nueces River, which meant it could have been washed down or drifted from just about anywhere. A coroner reckoned it to be snakebite, but because the body was decomposed it was not possible to be certain. Snakebite is the usual reason given for a death in Texas where the real reason for the cessation of life is not discernible.' She was suddenly very much the Pinkerton man then, giving her report to a fellow agent. All business, so I tried not to interrupt.

'The remains would have been buried where they were found and forgotten, were it not for the fact that two 20-dollar gold pieces were found in the pocket of the dead man's leather pants. The Ranger buried the body and handed the gold in to his captain who, in turn notified the federal authorities, and they in turn discovered the coins to be part of the vanished shipment, and it landed on the desk of Marshal Beaudine. Later a long-dead pony was found upstream and it was wearing the Doyle pitchfork brand of Purgatory.'

O'Bannion had earlier informed me that was the colourful name his associate had given to his property. 'That doesn't necessarily mean Doyle had anything to do with the missing gold or the dead Mexican.' She frowned at my interruption.

'True, but it was a place to start and when I discovered that a large section of the ranch had been posted, suspicions did direct themselves in his direction, either as a possible suspect in the original hijacking or of a subsequent discovery of the possible whereabouts of the gold. Either way, the Pinkerton Detective Agency got the contract and, at Beaudine's insistence, you got the job.'

'Have you ever met Doyle?' I asked in the silence that followed her background report.

'Doyle is a man to walk around, and he is rarely alone. Nearly always has that dreadful-looking man Elmore Cream at his side or one step behind. He will be curious of you as he was about me when I first arrived.'

'You talked with him?'

'He brought me here for supper on several occasions; we sat at this very table actually. He was always very respectful, but I could not help feeling he was thinking bad things.' She shuddered. 'My goodness, he is a fat man, he perspires freely. He always wears a white suit so in contrast with Cream who favours black. You will need to be very careful around either of them.'

'You are the second person today to tell me that.'

'O'Bannion?'

I nodded.

'Red is a sweet man. I feel he may have a troubled past he is trying to live down, but I trust him.'

'I think he feels a little guilty about his past, his early days,' I said.

'Fleeing Ireland, leaving the Mother Country when she was on her knees and at the mercy of the money men? Yes, that would be it. It is not an uncommon feeling. My own father shouldered that same guilt.'

'Why so many of you here in Dry Water?'

'We gather, we share a common bond, like the Italians and the Chinese, we gather.'

Again, that delightful chuckle and I could not help but hope I would hear more of it during my stay, no matter how brief that might be.

'Now, are you going to walk me home, Lucas Santana?'

* * *

Later that evening, back in my hotel room after a fine supper, seeing Kathleen to the door of the small house she rented and still wondering at the gentle kiss she had placed upon my cheek, I stared at the water-stained ceiling some more and tried to get the information she had given to me into some sort of order.

80

6

Black Bart and Me

The following day was mist-heavy, the warm early morning sun drying out the light shower of the overnight rain. I was up at first light and, before heading over to the Green Frog for breakfast, I called into the livery stable and asked the sleepy-eyed young lad to have the Morgan saddled and ready for me in half an hour. He stroked Bart; the dog had been waiting for me by the hotel door. I guess the animal saw me as his meal and booze ticket just so long as I was in town.

Breakfast stoked me up and Molly made me a packed lunch to which I added a bottle and some groceries from the general store. Kathleen Riley was not on duty in the millinery section and the *Bugle* office was locked, so I left her a note telling her I would be out of town for a couple of days. The Morgan was high on oats and frisky with it, and we left Dry Water at a fast trot. Before long we were out in the long grass country, our progress throwing up a rising of insects and the small colourful birds that feasted upon them. I was following as closely as I could to the map Kathleen had drawn for me. It was a countryside of several parts with a rocky high ground to the south and Mexico with dry, brush-covered arid land between the granite and the lush greenery of the pasture. Cottonwood and willow groves stretched each side of Dry Water Creek giving a healthy habitat to a variety of wildlife, mostly birds, but I also spotted several white-tailed deer and a skulking coyote, but very few cattle — and those few beeves all carried the Devil's pitch-fork brand of Doyle's Purgatory. There were several deserted homesteads and ancient diggings littering the landscape, filled, I supposed, with broken dreams and hearts. Here and there were more substantial buildings, one of which had suffered severe fire damage with only two walls and a stone chimney still standing, the stack pointing forlornly into the clear blue sky. There was a ragged raven's nest on the highest point of the chimney and I could hear the big bird calling close by, complaining about my intrusion. Now and again I caught sight of a distant rider and twice ran up against a barbed wire fence forcing me up to higher ground. I rode along it for a couple of miles, noting the frequency of the hand-painted signs warning that the land was private and intruders were likely to be shot. Texas friendly, I thought.

At around midday I settled by a small mountain creek whispering down a grey rock face and into a largish pool of clear cold water. I unsaddled the Morgan and hobbled her so she could wander a little and crop the nearby fresh green grass. I built a small fire and, with the line I had purchased in O'Bannion's store, I hooked two nice-sized crappies, which I gutted and smoked slowly on a homemade spit over hot wooden coals. I brewed some coffee and was just finishing washing plate and mug when a rider emerged from the nearby stand of cottonwoods. He was a cowhand from head to toe — young, shotgun, chaps, faded denims and light blue shirt, a wide-brimmed high-crowned Stetson and a sidearm he wore high on his hip. He studied me as carefully as I had studied him before speaking. 'Coffee sure smells good,' he said with a wide white-toothed smile.

'Step down, I was just about to toss it,' I said.

He smiled. 'Neighbourly of you.' He swung his leg easily out of the saddle and took the tin mug I offered, holding it with both hands and sipping the hot coffee.

'Stranger around these parts?'

'You could say that,' I said. 'Out of Dry Water, just getting the lay of the land.'

'Take care where you wander, mister, lot of this is private land.'

'And a lot of it is open range,' I said.

'Depends on your point of view,' he said.

'And what exactly is your point of view?' I asked.

'Don't have one, just a working hand pounding my backside for forty and found.' He put down his cup and drew his revolver as Bart emerged from the trees and made his way over to us.

'A damned dog,' he said, cocking the piece.

'You drop the hammer on that mutt and you are a dead man,' I said, very quietly.

He half turned toward me and I pulled fast, the muzzle of the Colt pointing directly at his belly button. He froze, then slowly lowered the hammer and holstered the gun.

'That was fast, mister, fastest I've ever seen.'

'And this is one of my slow days,' I said, letting a reassuring lightness into my tone.

'No problem, I didn't realize he was your animal.'

'He's not,' I said.

'Then why . . . ?'

I cut him off mid question. 'I believe I am his.'

The cowboy shook his head, trying to work that one through and coming up with, 'We have orders to shoot coyotes, cats and stray town dogs or any beef not wearing our brand.'

'Seems a bit extreme, especially as this is outside of your wire,' I said, spinning the gun on my finger and lodging it back in its holster in one easy show-off move, watching as Bart moved over to the fire and ate the discarded scraps of bread and fish.

'Mr Doyle, the owner, is a very private man.'

'Well he may just have to get used to me if I choose to run a few cows on a hundred and sixty acres of homestead land,' I said.

'Luck with that, mister,' he threw over his shoulder as he picked up the reins of his animal and remounted. I envied the ease with which his young body performed moves that were for me at times these days both painful and always an effort. 'Thanks for the coffee, maybe see you again sometime.'

'You can count on it, son.'

He turned and I watched until he had vanished into the tree line. 'You have to stop following me around, Bart. That's the second time I've saved your hide. You don't seem too popular and that might just rub off on me.'

If he cared, he didn't show it, but I knew that he knew right enough what I was saying. I have a way with animals.

* * *

That night I bedded down in one of the deserted homesteads, stabled the Morgan in a lean-to with some left-over hay and a couple of handfuls of grain I had packed in. Bart bellied down close to the door and, after carefully checking for snakes and scorpions, I rolled my blanket out on the floor and with my saddle for a pillow and a small fire in the broken-down but serviceable stove I slept fitfully through the thunder and the rain that the night had to offer.

7

My Dear Dead Companion

I arrived back in Dry Water in the late afternoon. The stable boy was pleased to see the Morgan and made a fuss of Bart. The dog had stayed close by me on the return journey. I gave the boy two bits and instruction to cut down on the oats. He nodded and handed me a note. 'Miss Riley asked me to give you that as soon as you got in. She says it's urgent.'

I thanked him and asked that he take my saddle gun and trappings over to the hotel for me when he had finished with the Morgan. I stepped out onto the street and opened the note, but before I could read it I saw her standing on the corner of Hood Street, which bisected the main thoroughfare roughly in the town centre. She was waving frantically and I made my way over to her.

As I reached her she looked at me and smiled a welcome, a smile that suddenly vanished as she looked over my shoulder, her fear-filled gaze fixed on something behind me. I heard the familiar zip of the bullet as it passed and then the report blending with the thud as it struck her above the left breast sending her body backwards onto the sidewalk. A second round passed her and clipped the hitching rail as I dived forward to cover her body with mine, pulling as I did so and, half turning, sent a round into the tall man in a long black duster standing in the shadow of the alleyway between the saloon and the bank. I saw the puff of dust and torn material pop from his shirt front just below his throat and drove another round in beside it. He staggered back and fell and I knew he was done. I set the smoking Colt on to the board near to her head and cradled her to me. There was a small weeping red hole in the yellow dress just above her left breast, but my knee beneath her back was soaked in blood from what I knew to be a large exit wound. Blood flecked her lips, as she gave me a smile — or was it a grimace; I had no way of telling. 'Dallas,' she whispered and then repeated the word 'Dallas . . . ' Her voice faded as the big darkness overtook her, and she died in my arms there on the dusty sidewalk of a no-account town in South Texas.

Redmond O'Bannion stepped forward and gently moved me away. 'I'll take care of it, son. You go check on your man down.'

'I'll take that gun, mister.' It was Max Hadley.

'Not on your best day,' I said, gently lowering her head and getting to my feet holstering the Colt as I did so.

'Leave it be, Max, I saw the whole thing. It was a back shooting, pure and simple.' It was O'Bannion and several voices in the gathering crowd echoed his words. I pushed past the deputy as he reluctantly gave way. I crossed the street to where the dead man lay spread-eagled, arms outstretched as if attempting to fly backwards. Two shots, neat holes clean through his throat, one of them, in all probability, breaking his neck as it passed through. I knelt down and went through his pockets. In his vest was a nickel watch with a sentiment and a name, James J. Watson of Baltimore. In his pockets a tattered letter, a bill of sale for a Purgatory horse, some loose change, a half-empty Bull Durham sack and that was it. Not a lot to show to make his worth dying for. His gun was nice, a new .45 Colt Army with a six and half inch barrel. I lowered the cocked hammer and slid it into its holster, a hand-tooled and expensive rig, then unbuckling the belt and rolling his body clear, I got to my feet as Hadley approached.

'What are you doing?'

'I like to know who I killed, deputy.' I tossed him the watch and the paper.

'And that sidearm?'

'A trophy,' I said bitterly. 'I usually take an ear or a trigger finger, but today I am not in the mood.' For a second time I pushed him out to of my way and wondered, as he stepped back, at the fire of hate in his eyes. Hate or frustration, I wondered which.

I crossed the street to where O'Bannion was still kneeling beside the dead Kathleen Riley. He crossed himself and made space for the doctor. 'When you've changed your pants,' he said, his voice almost a whisper and nodding to the blood-soaked Levi's, 'drop by for a special when you have a mind to.' The Irish in his voice stronger than usual, a special kinship with the dead woman perhaps.

I nodded and made my way back to the hotel and up to my room. I tossed the gunbelt onto the bed, hung my own rig over the brass bedhead and poured myself a shot of whiskey, remembering the bottle I had so recently shared with Kathleen Riley. After washing and changing my pants, I turned my attention to the gunman's rig. The gun was a .45

Colt Army cavalry model, blued steel and in superb condition. I studied on it for some time before I emptied the remaining three rounds from cylinder and slid it back into the reinforced leather of the holster, and I was about to place it in the bureau drawer when I noticed a small slit in the soft pigskin inner lining of the tooled leather, close to where the holster slid along the belt. I widened the slit with my folding knife, poked inside the lining and pulled out two mint 20-dollar double eagle gold pieces.

★   ★   ★

I lay on the bed for a long time that evening staring up at the now familiar ceiling, trying to make a recognizable shape from the brown water stain, the untouched drink beside me, and holding the memory of the passed hours clearly in my head. Death was not an unusual thing for me to be around, but other than the memory of the long ago dead young Yankee soldier and Darryl J.

Jones I did not dwell on thoughts of those I had killed or of friends who had died and yet I had the dreadful feeling that the passing of Kathleen Riley, a comrade in arms, would haunt me for the rest of my days.

An insistent knocking at the door broke my reverie and, removing my gun from its holster and keeping it in my hand beneath the patchwork quilt, I yelled for whoever it was to come in. The door opened cautiously and the bespectacled bald head of the desk clerk poked around the corner.

'Excuse me, sir, but that damned dog that followed you over is howling outside of the door. If he don't quit or go away I will have to call the sheriff.'

'Let him up here,' I said.

'We don't allow dogs in the hotel, sir.'

'You do now,' I said, letting him see the gun. 'And you call the deputy, I'll put out your light for all time.' Talking tough sometimes gets the job done, and I can talk hard when I need to.

He closed the door and moments

later opened it again and Bart came in, jumped up onto the bed beside me and, resting his head on my knee, went to sleep.

8

Target Practice

I awoke with a dry throat and an aching back. The dog was snoring on the floor by the door and it was well past first light. I washed, dressed in a clean shirt, parcelled up my dirty laundry for the Chinaman to collect as arranged with the desk clerk, and with Bart at my heels made my way downstairs and along to the Green Frog. Molly set a breakfast in front of me with a sad smile, her hand gentle on my shoulder as she passed by and returned with a bowl of scraps, which she took outside for the waiting mutt. 'Kathy used to feed him here most days, so I guess he's your responsibility now.'

I finished breakfast and asked her for a pencil and some notepaper with an envelope if she had one. Sipping my third cup of coffee, I wrote a brief but succinct note to the head of the San Antonio office, not wanting to send a wire and risking revealing myself to the telegrapher. That would be a risk in this small community where secrets would be few and far between. The dispatcher at the stage depot told me I had missed the morning mail, but if it was urgent I could catch up with the morning stage at the Del Moro swing station if I rode cross country, which halved the distance of the stage route. I did that, told the dog to stay and headed east at a fast clip, arriving at Del Moro five minutes before the Overland Stage. I gave the letter to the manager, who stamped it and dropped it into the mail sack and sealed it.

'Just in time, friend,' then adding, 'It's a sure enough fine morning.'

I thanked him. 'Every morning is fine,' I said.

'Yes, it sure enough is,' he said. 'Here she comes now. See the dust? Letter will be in San Antonio by morning. It is a sure enough service, no worries about downed wires and loose-mouthed telegraphers.' He laughed at some hidden meaning, but I sure enough guessed what he meant. Lonely country folk can be sure enough strange.

I rested the Morgan for an hour and then headed back the way I had come, wondering what the reaction to Agent Riley's death would be. The funeral was to be on Saturday, so being Thursday gave the office two days to contact me with further instructions or to pull me out. They could pull all they wanted, but I would not quit this case until the paymaster behind the 20-dollar gold pieces was dead and buried. Something at the back of my mind was struggling to come forward.

The gentle motion of the sure-footed Morgan as we crossed the open countryside lulled me almost to sleep but I awoke, suddenly awakened by the imagined sound of yesterday's gunfire, the two rounds racketing past me followed suddenly by the silence and I knew exactly what that hidden thought was. The closely placed shots of yesterday were still rolling through my troubled mind, and then it became clear.

★ ★ ★

My first stop was the hotel and my room. There I shucked my own sidearm and strapped on the killer's rig; it fitted like a glove. I checked the cylinder and loaded five rounds, leaving the hammer to rest on the empty chamber as was the custom, considering the single-action Colt had no safety catch. Back in the street I retrieved two empty bean cans from the hotel's trash and headed the Morgan south to the rocky Dry Water Creek a mile from town. I looked back and considered the misty distance to be adequate and dismounted, tying the horse off to a dead mesquite bush. I set the two cans one behind the other on a flat rock and paced off thirty yards roughly the width of Dry Water's Main Street. I turned and deliberately aimed the weapon at the rear of the two cans clearly visible. I squeezed off a round. The can span off into the air. I retrieved it and reset it a little further behind the front can and fired again and again it was a hit. I repeated this twice more, each time moving the rear can a little further behind the front can. The fourth shot barely scratched the visible slither of can, merely dislodging it. I tried a fifth and last round just to be certain and got the same result. The Colt was a superbly accurate weapon, honed to perfection and the extra couple of inches to the barrel length improved its accuracy considerably. I holstered the empty gun and headed back to Dry Water clearing my thoughts of any doubt along the way.

★ ★ ★

O'Bannion was in the saloon sipping coffee at the bar and reading the San Antonio newspaper left for him by the morning's stage. He looked up, gave me a tired smile. 'Coffee, Rivers?'

'That would be good,' I said. 'And for the record my given name is Lucas Santana. If you have heard of me, forget all you have heard.'

He gave me a puzzled look and yelled, 'Jerry, bring me a fresh pot of coffee and another mug, won't you.' He turned back to me. 'No, never heard of you. Should I have?'

The wizened little relief bartender brought in a tray, nodded to me, set it on the bar and returned to his chores in the backroom.

'You've been gone all day. Anything I should know about?'

'Only this, Red.' I pulled the Colt, double-checked it was empty and handed it to him. 'Look at it. Tell me, what do you see?'

I sipped the hot coffee and watched as the big Irishman examined the weapon. Dry firing it once to check the pull and half cocking it, he rolled the cylinder full circle. 'A beautiful piece if you can ever call such a killing machine beautiful. Have I missed something here, though?'

'Look at the back strap. What do you see?'

He took a pair of wire-rimmed spectacles from his vest pocket, smiled apologetically over them, and returned his attention to the Colt. 'I see a capital E and J followed by Hartford, Connecticut, and a number I cannot quite make out. Should that mean something to me?'

'Does it?'

'It should do, something familiar about it. Give me a minute.' He studied the back strap again. 'Hartford, a Colt factory gunsmith's mark?'

'Not a gunsmith's mark, Red — *the* gunsmith's mark. That piece has been hand-tooled and finished by a master craftsman, a German by the name Erich Jürgen, one of the best there is.'

'And this means what?'

'It means that I wasn't the target and John J. Watson of Baltimore hit what he was aiming at. I tried that beast out by the creek this afternoon and it only hits what it is aimed at.'

O'Bannion stared at me in disbelief, my words sinking in with obvious effect. 'Why?' His voice was a whisper husky with emotion. 'Why the hell would anyone want to harm our Kathleen? Everyone liked her. She has only been here six months or so, and I never heard a bad word said about her. She was one of us, for God's sake.'

'She was a newspaperman; newspaper folk make enemies. Any idea if she was working on anything controversial?'

He thought for a long moment. 'Nothing I can think of. Small town, small town news. She talked to a lot of people, different backgrounds, a little gossip to whet the appetites of the ladies but no, nothing that I can think of as might get someone riled up enough to do her harm.'

'Do you have a key to the *Bugle*'s office?'

'I have a key to practically every building in Dry Water. Why?'

'Let's go take a look-see. Maybe she was working on something for a future issue,' I said. There was a note of desperation in my voice or an urgency I could not give voice to.

The *Bugle*'s office was like any other you could find in any such establishment: banks of paper, discarded ink-stained sleeve protectors, printing blocks and the cast iron press with its large printing plate. We spent a long two hours searching through Kathleen's many hand-written notes, outlines for articles, layouts and future editorials and came up with nothing more than you would expect from a small town local newspaper. There was a note on the desk telling Jason Preston, her printer, that she would be late in the morning as she was on duty in the general store until noon.

'You know Preston?' I asked.

'Yes, everyone does, nice old guy, smallest man in town, a long-time print man. He came out of retirement just to help her out when her company bought up the newspaper, which had not seen an issue for several years.'

'Do you know who owns the paper now?' I asked.

'No idea, some outfit in San Antonio, I think. Do you know?'

'Nothing here to help us,' I said, ignoring the question.

'No, nothing here to even show where she came from,' O'Bannion said. 'Nothing personal here, no reference to anyone other than local people. We know she didn't have a suitor in town; many tried, but were swiftly rejected.'

'She had a lover in San Antonio,' I said.

'She did? How do you know that?'

'She told me.'

'Told you? Why would she do that?'

'Animals trust me; people also — they tell me things,' I said, and we left it at that and walked slowly back to the Tavern. It had filled up in our absence and the evening after-supper crowd were involved in their usual banter although, I thought to myself, it was somewhat subdued and guessed that the death of Kathleen Riley and the shooting of John J. Watson on their Main Street had a profound impact on the good people of Dry Water.

We bellied up to the bar and O'Bannion signalled to Jerry for an under-the-counter bottle of his best Irish, and carrying it and two shot glasses, we retired to a corner table.

'Do you have some bigger stake in this, Lucas Santana, or were you just an unfortunate bystander?'

I did not answer directly but dropped a question of my own. 'Dallas, does the town have any connections to Dallas?'

'Hell no, we are closer to San Antonio than Dallas on horseback or by the Overland. You only go to Dallas if you want to ride the rails east. I have never been there in all the years I have lived here. Why do you ask?'

'When I was holding her, when she was dying, 'Dallas' was all she said, and she said it twice as if it was important to her and should be to me.' It was awkward for me talking to O'Bannion that way, not telling him the full story, playing him. But I had no choice, disclosing my relationship with the dead woman would put me at a disadvantage and that was a risk I was not prepared to take.

'How come you were so close to her all of a sudden?'

'We shared the dog,' I said.

'It's a mystery,' was all O'Bannion had left to offer.

'Is Hadley going to question Danny Doyle?' I asked, feeling almost as frustrated as the big Irishman.

'Why would he do that? Watson wore a black duster, but they are not uncommon and although the bill of sale for the horse shows it was bought from Doyle, that in itself means nothing. Doyle sells horses to a good many people, including me, so that is a dead end. I can pressure the deputy because I have a good relationship with the county sheriff, but I can only push him so far.' He sounded resigned to the fact.

I said goodnight, took supper at the Green Frog and, with Bart at my heel, returned to the hotel. The clerk gave me a mean look as we crossed the lobby but he quickly vanished into the back room when the dog looked in his direction.

109

9

Joshua Beaufort

The next day, Friday, I continued my reconnoitre of the surrounding countryside and learned very little. I fancied I would learn a great deal more were I to cross the wire, but I was not yet ready for that. I arrived back in Dry Water in time to meet the evening Overland and joined the usual group of loafers who gathered to see who was on board and in the hope of collecting their mail.

First out was a red-faced drummer wearing a chequered fawn suit and brown derby hat. He clutched a sample bag close to his chest, but still managed to catch another bag tossed down to him by the stage's shotgun. He was followed closely by Joshua Beaufort. I recognized him straight away. He was a war veteran and top Pinkerton under-cover operative in south and west Texas, a tall, handsome man with an impressive grey moustache and sideburns to match. He wore a tailored tan frock-coated suit and only the very slight bulge under his left arm told me he was packing. I wondered idly if Deputy Hadley would notice it, but assumed not. In any event, it made no matter, Beaufort would never go anywhere or do anything without a thorough intelligence briefing and that was where we fell out that one time we had met in the Big Bend country.

We had met on that one case and, for the most part, we had rubbed along quite well. There had been a few minor differences of opinion, but on the whole we agreed that short cuts were sometimes necessary and taking a half step beyond the law in order to reach a desired outcome was not the end of the world for either of us.

Water under the bridge and Del Rio was five years behind, time enough for the both of us to grow old and learn. The last time I saw him, he had presented me with a fine Henry repeating rifle, which sits in my gun rack back in Wyoming. It was a rifle he 'liberated' along with many others from a notorious gunrunner during the Civil War at a time he was attached to Allan Pinkerton's Washington staff.

Josh Beaufort was in company with a middle-aged woman, dark-skinned with long black hair, handsome with strong features and a gentle smile for the loafer who caught her bag and carried it into the hotel for her. Beaufort winked at me as he passed by but that was the only acknowledgement he gave to my presence, and even that was more than I had expected given the situation.

★　★　★

The next morning O'Bannion joined me at the breakfast table, he sat down with a great sigh and stared at me. His eyes were troubled.

'Problem, Red?' I asked, as I wiped up the last remnants of my three-egg meal with crisp sourdough bread and washed it down with hot coffee.

'Mayoral problems, my friend, the burdens of office. Seems the owner of the *Bugle* came in on the evening stage yesterday, along with a possible replacement editor. He called on my office this morning and cancelled the funeral. Kathleen is to be shipped back to San Antonio by special freight starting out tonight, for interment in her family plot. Undertaker is in a stew about it worrying he might lose his fee and the state of his cold room, and Preacher Holt is pissed as well; seems he had a nice service all planned out. Major Allen, he's the owner by the way, calmed them down some, and there will be a church service this afternoon for local people to pay their respects and his eulogy will be heard. Santana, I swear sometimes I do not understand people at all.'

'That's why I get on so well with

animals. They are trouble sometimes but far less complicated. You always know where you stand with a western diamondback, but sometimes it is very difficult to read people, folk who can bite you in the ass just as easily.'

'Bit too profound for me this early in the morning. You coming to the service with me?'

'No, sir,' I said quietly, 'I have my own memories of Kathleen Riley and I don't want to share them with a crowd of bible thumpers and hearse chasers.'

'Bit hard don't you think? She was well-liked, one fine lady.'

I got to my feet, pushed back the chair and dropped a dollar on to the table. 'Things without all remedy should be without regard: what's done, is done.'

He stared up at me.

'*Macbeth*,' I threw over my shoulder as I walked away. Like I said, I am well-read.

★ ★ ★

Outside the street was quiet and I paused to roll my first cigarette of the day, telling myself, as I did every morning, that I had to quit. No doubt it was bad for me, and my wife hated the smell of tobacco on my breath. I promised myself there and then that when I rode out of Dry Water, I would leave the makings on O'Bannion's polished bar. I turned left and made my way toward the livery stable, passing as I did so the drummer. He was gazing sadly at the sign on the *Bugle*'s door telling the reader it was closed and why. I have no idea what caused me to pause but I did. Maybe it was the sadness in his pale eyes; sad drummers do not thrive in the West. 'She was a fine lady,' I said. He looked at me, a forlorn look, something extra sad about it, worried; it prompted me to linger.

'You knew her?' he asked.

'Yes,' I said, 'we were friends.'

He looked at my sidearm, and then up at me. 'You the gun that shot her killer?'

I nodded.

'Well then, you had best have this, no one else to give it to.' He opened his bag and took out a half-pint bottle of whiskey and handed it to me. 'Twenty-year-old Irish malt. It's a special item bought and paid for.'

'Kathleen bought a twenty-year-old bottle of Irish whiskey?'

'Not for herself, son, it was for that old warthog Hector the Hooch — you know him?'

'No,' I said.

'Looks like a dead tree branch, a brown, withered and weathered old stick, runs a still around here somewhere up in the hill country, does me out of business. She bought it for him. I'm leaving on the morning stage so you can drink it yourself or find him. Either way it saddens me I could not give it to her myself.'

'I'll find him,' I said.

'Thought you might.' He held out his hand and I took it. 'Thanks for getting the snake, son, and don't you lose any sleep over killing him.'

I watched him walk away thinking, *Hector the Hooch, colourful.*

* * *

I heard the distant church bell clang. The Morgan was grazing close by, dragging her grounded reins as she munched and moved among the tall, fresh green grass and stream water. Bart was nowhere to be seen and O'Bannion told me later that the dog had stationed himself outside of the church for the whole of the service, letting out an occasional howl, and that he had restrained Hadley from hurting the animal or moving him on. Dogs have a right to mourn, he had told the man. The sun warmed me and I slept with my back against a live oak and waited. After a couple of hours, I saw a dust cloud and from it appeared the livery's rental buggy. I waited as it drew near, then turned off from the trail toward where the Morgan was flopped out on her side. She struggled to her feet as the buggy approached and stopped three yards in front of me. She paused, then went over to the pulling horse and did what horses do.

Joshua Beaufort climbed down and, holding his partner's arm, walked over to me. We shook hands and he introduced me to his companion. 'This beautiful lady is my wife Lorena. Lorena, I want you to meet the Peaceful River Kid.'

She smiled and shook my hand. 'Heard a lot about you, Lucas, and not all of it good.'

I laughed.

Two miles out of town and westerly; that was always the arrangement for clandestine meetings. If Beaufort had not come today, then he would have come tomorrow; and if not then, it would be up to me to go find him. It was routine and it worked. It had certainly worked in Del Rio.

We made idle conversation for a while. Sometimes we were quiet, thinking maybe of absent friends, smoking, sharing the picnic they had brought and the cold beer in a stone jar. We could have gone on for hours that way talking around the death of a fellow agent, but it had to be faced sometime.

'You have any thoughts as to the why of it?' Beaufort eventually asked me.

'No, I was hoping you might shed some light on it for me. I have no idea. We had only just made firm contact, but I liked her right from the get-go. A straight ace lady. Folk thought and still do that I was the target. The local law is a piece of crap — my apologies, ma'am.'

'We are all Pinkerton men here, Lucas. Talk like we are,' she said. 'I hear worse at home from time to time.'

'Major Allen, newspaperman,' I said. 'A nice touch. I like it.'

It was the alias Allan Pinkerton used during the Civil War.

'Do you believe it has anything to do with this case, anything at all?' she asked.

'In all honesty, I am not sure. She

may have upset some of the locals, but to hire a gunman of Watson's standing is unlikely. Hell, it was only a local gossip rag really and she did take it lightly, I thought.'

'Pinkerton was about to close this line of enquiry as a dead end, but now he is not so sure. What are your thoughts on this, Lucas?' Beaufort asked.

I did not answer right away. Something, some little possibly unimportant thing, was niggling away at me. Nothing tangible; just a feeling. I had bet my life on such feelings many times and I am still walking. I know for a fact that Beaufort felt the same and would back me whatever I said, even if it meant going against the wishes of our employer. 'Truth to tell, I have no concrete thoughts on this, Josh, but you remember that time in Del Rio when your young partner Jake Benbow was blindsided, and I pulled and shot the fat drummer who had fired a hideaway from inside his cloak? Even you thought I was crazy, but I knew there was something wrong with that man and taking him down probably saved your hide and mine, as well as Benbow's. You remember you asked me how I knew and I had no answer for you, I just knew. People were calling for my blood, but you rolled him over and it really was a smoking gun case and it was still cocked in his cold, dead hand. You remember that?'

Beaufort looked at Lorena and said, 'How could I ever forget it.' It wasn't a question.

She smiled up at him and then at me. 'I did not know that. Thank you, Lucas.'

Beaufort got to his feet. 'You got that feeling again, haven't you.'

Again, it was not a question, but I nodded anyway.

'OK we will run with it. Keep in close touch, use the telegraph in brief standard code, only use the Overland if it is a lengthy enquiry, you know the drill. Lorena was going to take over the *Bugle*, but I think it best we leave it be. I will clear this with the old man, let's

121

get it done. Anyone in Dry Water you can trust?'

'O'Bannion, the saloon keeper, he has been around forever. He's bored and keeps his thoughts to himself. Kathleen liked him and I think I can trust him.'

'I can send Jacob Benbow when he has about finished trying to run down Jesse James, but that may take a while yet.'

'No need, I can handle it.'

'Good luck then, Lucas, we'll be in touch.' We shook hands and I tipped my hat to Lorena.

I watched them out of sight thinking of them together and wondering what Annie Blue was doing back on our Wildcat ranch in Wyoming.

10

A Bottle of Old Irish

It was evening on the Monday following the Sunday of Kathleen Riley's church service. The storm clouds had gathered throughout the day and I had spent most of it loafing and listening. It is surprising just how much you can learn about the comings and goings of small town folk by doing just that. Sitting in the Green Frog, the Bullhorn Cantina or playing a solitary game of billiards in O'Bannion's back room. Listening and loafing, I became part of the furniture, ignored by most. Everything you need to know for background is out there. You just have to go and find it and I did. But not, as it happens, by that particular method, but rather completely by accident in conversation with O'Bannion in the empty Tavern later that evening.

I took an early supper at the Green Frog, drank my coffee and thanked Molly for a paper bag filled with bones and scrap for Bart, and headed back to the hotel to study the ceiling some more while trying to make sense of the Dallas connection and wondering how much I should tell O'Bannion. When I had told Beaufort the man could be trusted, I had meant it. Problem for me was not wanting to push the old man into the path of any shit storm that might blow up if the Dry Water connection and the stolen gold proved to be viable. My attention eventually wandered to the bureau and the bottle of twenty-year-old Irish sitting there. That seemed to be one problem I could deal with. Strapping on my gunbelt in the hope I would run into Max Hadley and piss the man off some more, now that would make my evening. There was an aggression in me that needed tending. I made my way downstairs past the sleeping Bart who had stationed himself at the doorway in order, I believe, to piss off the desk clerk, who ignored my attempt at a smile. That dog and I were both ornery at times and that's for sure. I crossed the street, the light eerie in the misty rain, the guttering oil lamps flickering in the stiff breeze, their shadowy intermittent glow lighting my way to the Tavern.

Monday, it was quiet, probably the quietest evening ever in any cow town anywhere. I pushed open the slatted doors and stepped into the lamp-lit gloom. There were no customers to disturb the freshly saw-dusted floor and the only living soul in the large room was a tired-looking O'Bannion at a table close to the bar, a dead pipe in the corner of his mouth and a deck of red Bicycle playing cards in front of him laid out for solitaire. He looked up smiled, pleased to see me I thought.

'Pull up a chair, son. I'll get us a drink.' He started to get to his feet, but I waved him down and passing him went behind the bar, retrieved a pair of shot glasses and set them down on the table in front of him. He stared at them then looked up at me. 'We just going to pretend to drink?'

I fished the bottle of whiskey out from the inside pocket of my jacket and set it on the table. He looked at it and then up at me and then back down again at the bottle. He slipped on his eyeglasses, which were suspended on a leather thong about his neck, and picked up the bottle, reading the label and then carefully setting the bottle back down. 'Christmas has come early! Been a long while since I set my green eyes on one of those, sir, the stuff that dreams are made of. Where did you find such a fine bottle of the Irish?'

'The whiskey drummer who came into town on the Friday's Overland gave it me.'

'And why would he do that? It's worth more than a dollar or two to a homesick old man.' The Irish in his voice was suddenly much more pronounced. I liked the sound of it.

'He brought it in for Kathleen Riley. She ordered it some time back for a friend. A present, I'm guessing.' I picked up the bottle. 'To drink it or not to drink it, that is the question.'

'You, it seems, have already taken up arms against a sea of troubles, so perhaps we should go ahead and drink it.' He gave me a broad smile. 'You are not the only one around here who has read a book or two.'

'Should we, though? It is not really ours. Perhaps we are merely the keepers?'

'You know who it was for then?' He licked his lips and picked up the bottle again.

'Yes, but I have no idea who he is.'

'You have a name?' He set the bottle back down.

'One Hector the Hooch.'

'Jesus H, I know she felt something for that old rummy. He told her a story or two, made her laugh.' He paused. 'She had a lovely laugh, didn't she.' It was an observation not a question. We were both quiet for a while. Finally, he added, 'She always bought him a meal when he was in town.'

'You know him well?'

'Certainly I do. Old goat runs a still out in the piney-woods back up by Three Falls, sells it to the locals and the Cantina sells it cheap to the Mexicans and broke cowhands. Damned forty-rod hooch, bust-head, lights a fire inside of you in winter and blows your head off in summer.'

'He an Irishman?'

'More Irish than most, still talks the old language. Strange considering his name, more Germanic than Irish.'

'His name is German?'

'Well maybe not German, but certainly not Irish. Dulles, it is Hector Dulles, least that's what it says on his mail when he gets any.'

I stared at O'Bannion and he stared right back and we both spoke at the same time, exactly the same words.

'Dulles, Dallas . . .'

'Close up, get the keys,' I said. 'I

want another closer look at the *Bugle* office, we may have been looking for the wrong thing last time.'

He didn't move, looking at me, waiting. 'Who the hell are you, Santana?'

I did not hesitate. 'I work for the Pinkerton Detective Agency and so did Kathleen Riley.'

★ ★ ★

Some waters just simply feel good and you know that wherever you drop your hooked line, the bobber will jump and the fish will be in the pan before sunset. Then again, sometimes those attractive waters have already been fished clean and you can cut bait all day long and never get a bite. The *Bugle* was the latter. We searched every nook and cranny, every possible place where the big fish might be lurking, but we fished in vain. I flopped down in Kathleen's big chair and O'Bannion drew up the spare and settled in front of me. We looked at each other and shook our heads. I popped the cork of a near full bottle of whiskey I found in one of the desk drawers and we drank from the neck passing the bottle to and fro in silence.

'Dulles must know something,' I said. 'It has to be something he told Kate, something she felt important enough to whisper to me when she was so badly holed. I had better ride out and talk with him. Can you draw me a map?'

'Better yet, I could take you there.'

'No, Red, you are already likely in over your head. Best you spend as little time in my company as possible. I don't need you on my conscience.'

He nodded. 'It's about a half day's ride, partly covering the ground you already covered, but coming up short of Doyle's wire and turning for higher ground. I rode up there one time, the old coot damn nearly took my head off with an old trapdoor Springfield. His cabin is up in the foothills close by where three little falls, big after a rain like this but still of little consequence, merge just above a place we call Indian Rock and then run on down to join Dry Water Creek. The Rock is tall, shaped a bit like a head with a thin feather at the summit, you can't miss it. No idea where the still is, but it must be close by and he will know you are coming long before you see him.'

'That it?'

'More or less. I'll draw you a map tonight. You can pick it up in the morning, and take that damned dog with you. Keep him out of my way. Since you've been in town, the mutt thinks he owns the place and besides, Hector likes him.'

'I'll do that. Can you tidy up here a bit tomorrow? It belongs to Pinkerton now.'

'Sure, I will get Jerry on it.'

I told him most of what there was to know, impressed upon him the need for his silence, killed the bottle and left the *Bugle*'s office to Kathleen Riley, whose presence we had both been aware of but neither had spoken of it.

131

11

Hector the Hooch

A half hour after sunrise I was three miles out from Dry Water, riding easy through the long grass that bounded several miles each side of Dry Water Creek, lush range that slowly turned to scrub as we reached the rolling foothills and began to make higher ground through stands of ponderosa pine and rocky gullies. But always gaining a little higher ground. Bart kept close by and from time to time I spotted a rider keeping abreast, but moving on if I turned the Morgan in his direction. Apart from songbirds, jays and carrion crows, wildlife was sparse and from the number of animal carcases we passed, I guessed that what the young cowhand had told me was true. A dead unbranded steer, a dog, several coyotes and even a big cat were evidence to that fact. The dog, the coyotes and cougar were strung up by their hind legs and left to rot in the lower branches of scrub oak. It sickened me and tainted any idea I had as to just who or what Doyle was. There was no real definable trail and O'Bannion had told me that Hector packed his hooch down by mule in barrels and transferred the raw moonshine to jugs courtesy of the Cantina's owner, Cherry Vargas. The higher ground was given over to more pinions and odd clearings of grass showing ample sign of deer, so I supposed we were well clear of Doyle's wire and nearing the home of one Hector Dulles.

O'Bannion had made it clear to me that Hector could be a little unstable and that I should take care. He was old but quick on his feet, and had for many years outwitted the federal authorities in their quest to extract their share of tax revenue from the old man's income. Bart saw him first. The dog stopped dead in his tracks, blocking the Morgan's way through a narrow cleft in the rocks just short of Indian Head, which was easy to see and just as O'Bannion had described it. The dog lay down, poised, and I reined the Morgan in and waited. I could not see the man, but I could smell him; I have a keen sense of smell. It was not an unpleasant odour — more of a musky smell, like an old book, something old, worn but not unclean. Hector Dulles stepped out less than ten feet in front of Bart, a hefty Trapdoor Springfield rifle pointing unwaveringly at my chest. He was exactly as the drummer had described him, an old, weathered stick of a man, rail thin, worn buckskins hanging loosely on his lean frame, a battered top hat on his narrow head, long hair pouring out from under the brim like a grey river.

'You a revenue man?' His voice was soft, more Irish than any other I had heard in Dry Water. I noted the hammer of the rifle was eared back to full cock.

'No, sir,' I said. 'I most certainly am not.'

'Where'd you get the dog?'

Bart had not moved and even belly down his tail was wagging, beating the grass.

'I didn't. He kind of got me.' I said.

'What are you doing up here?'

'Came to see you.'

'What the hell you want to see me for?'

'Brought you a gift, a gift from a friend. You lower that Springfield's hammer and let me get it from my saddle-bag, I'll give it to you.'

He lowered the hammer but the muzzle of the gun did not waver. I shifted my weight in the saddle and reached back into my saddle-bag and extracted the bottle of Irish. 'Catch,' I said, tossing it to him. He caught it in one hand and still the rifle's muzzle did not waver.

'From Miss Riley?' he asked, staring first at the bottle then up at me and finally at Bart. He set the Springfield and the whiskey down against a rock and tapped his thigh. The dog moved swiftly to him, licking the old man's face as he stooped to greet him.

'A real fine lady. How is she?'

'She's dead,' I said. 'Shot to death on Dry Water's Main Street by a coward name of James J. Watson, late of Baltimore.'

His face showed no expression, no emotion, the tired green eyes transfixed on the dog. He did not acknowledge my words.

'She was also a friend of mine,' I said. 'I shot and killed the man who gunned her down.'

He slowly straightened, picked up the rifle and the bottle and turned his back on me. 'Follow me. Your horse can stable with my mules. I'll fix us some grub. The dog's welcome. We'll have us a drink.' Then he was gone, moving swiftly over the rough ground ahead of me, a line of us — Hector, the dog and me. It began to rain and lightning danced along the low ridge and thunder rattled amongst the pines, raising the hackles on Bart's neck.

★ ★ ★

136

The cabin with its corral and lean-to was set on the edge of a small expanse of grassland, with a scattering of pine and aspen trees and one old, long-ago lightning-struck, blackened live oak that with its few leafed branches was still clinging to life. The cabin was built with unsawed lumber. It had two windows, both of which were glazed and both had thick tarpaulin drop-down curtains for protection if the weather got too violent, cold or wet. The inside smelled a bit like the old man, musty. It was spartan but functional — a big stove that must have taken a lot of hauling up to that meadow, a sink with an iron pump, cupboards, two bunks, a wood table and a couple of old barroom chairs. The stove was alight and a large pan burbled on the open top.

Hector pointed to the bunk furthest away from the stove. 'You can bed down there. Too stormy to travel back tonight. There's a crapper out back. The dog can sleep with the animals or in here if you want. I don't mind either way.'

'Thanks,' I said. 'Bart can make up his own mind. I'll go see to my horse.'

'Bring your saddle, blanket and bedroll in. I don't have any spare bedding and don't get any visitors either so that makes no matter. You like rabbit stew? I hope so, it's all I got anyway.'

'Suits me fine,' I said, and meant it.

★   ★   ★

We ate our meal in silence. It was good food; the old man could cook. He had made dumplings, added carrots and spuds and a host of fresh meadow herbs. I could not fault it. He cleared away his plate, but ladled more into mine and put it by the door for Bart who cleared it in seconds.

We sat across from each other. He refused a stogie, saying he preferred his pipe, which he filled, tamped and fired, its fragrance filling the room, warming it in a way a log fire on its own can never do. The bottle of Irish sat in the middle of the table along with two preserve jars. He stared at it, reached over, opened it, poured two generous shots and raised his glass to the light, staring at the rich amber liquid lit by the glow of one of the two oil lamps. '*Sláinte*, my darlin' Kathleen,' he said quietly and downed the drink in one long swallow. 'I'll take longer with the second shot,' he said, with a sad smile, noting that I had only sipped mine. It was exquisitely rich and full-bodied, but as smooth as silk.

'To Kathleen,' I said, and sipped some more.

'You a newspaperman like she was, mister? Hell, I don't even know your name.'

'Lucas Santana, and yes we were in the same business.' I sensed he had no love for the law, any law, so thought it best to do what I do best — lie.

'How'd you know about me?'

'We were very close. I knew her friends in San Antonio. We worked for the same man, shared our stories.'

He topped up our jars and studied on

me for some long minutes. 'But that don't rightly mean you would ride all of this way just to deliver a bottle of Irish, as fine and rare as it may be.'

'That is true, Hector, but we were working on the same story and she died in my arms saying your name. That meant a lot to her, so it means a lot to me.'

'It's the gold, isn't it? That damned gold story she was so excited about when I saw her last week, day before she died I reckon.' He got to his feet and walked over to the sideboard, his heavy work boots raising little puffs of dust that sparkled and lingered in the air. He opened the drawer, reached inside and returned to the table. He was holding a small soft leather pouch, which he tossed on to the table in front of me. 'That's what got her killed, I wouldn't wonder.'

I picked up the pouch, undid the drawstring and tipped the 20-dollar double eagle onto the table. I did not touch it, but leaned back in my chair and looked from it to him and waited. I did not want to question him or lead him in any way. If he wanted to tell me, he would; if he did not, then all the questions in the world would not make the slightest bit of difference.

'Is that what she died for, Lucas Santana, one fucking double eagle?'

'It is very possible, Hector. But not for the one coin, but the story behind it, where you found it, who knew about it. It's the story that killed her, not a 20-dollar gold piece.'

'Can I keep it?'

'Yes, as far as I am concerned, I have no interest in the coin. All I will say is, spend it a long way from here.'

'You need to know what I told her. You want I should tell it to you? You willing to die for a story in a two-bit newspaper in a one-horse town like Dry Water? I don't think so, Santana.'

I let the silence in the room be overtaken by the sudden rattle of the rain on the board roof and the rolling thunder in the hills around the cabin. I sipped my drink and lit another stogie. His pale green eyes never once left my face, reading me like I was a book, reaching the last page and deciding whether he had enjoyed it or even understood it.

'Were you in the war, Santana? You must have been very young if you were.'

'I'm older than I look.'

'North or South?'

'John Hood's Texas Brigade.'

'I thought so, you got army writ all over you. Newspaperman my ass, you are a lawman now. Federal, the rangers, or are you still army?'

I didn't see any point in lying to him further. 'I mostly work for a private detective agency sometimes out of the San Antonio office, but not always. Kathleen was my partner and I aim to kill the man behind the man who gunned her down. That's not what I am being paid to do, but it's what partners do and she would have done the same thing for me.'

'You are looking for that missing gold

shipment they talk about?'

'We were and I will.'

'I believe you in that, and I may be of some help. Not for you but for her. She treated me well and I can forgive both of you the deceit if your lives were on the line. We'll finish this fine bottle of the Irish and in the morning I will show you the cave where I found the coin, but I will not go in there with you, no, not ever again, not for all the gold in California.'

★ ★ ★

We were once again in single file, Hector on his mule, me on the Morgan and Bart at our heels. The morning air was fresh and clean after the rain and the smell of the burnt ozone lingered and became stronger as we made the higher ground. After an hour or so, the old man raised a hand and stopped close by a steep grey granite bluff, the base of which was covered in high scrub, mostly a mixture of mesquite and blackbrush, but all of it thorn-laden. The brush began where the grass ended. He pointed to the base of the cliff about a hundred yards in front of us.

'Fight your way through that and you will find a cave. Here.' He handed me the oil lantern he had packed on the mule. 'You will need this. They call it Whistling Rock, a strange noise inside there. Whites say it is the wind, but the Tonkawa say it's the lost spirits of the dead bound to this earth and finding no way home. You take your pick, lawman, but I been in there and I'm not about to go again. No sir, not me, not this child.'

'You believe in ghosts, old man?'

'It's the Irish in me. See how you feel when you see what I seen. I'll be here waiting on you coming out, that is if you do come out.' He smiled at that and turned the mule and led the Morgan and Bart back to the grass.

I made my way afoot up the last of the incline and stopped by the thick brush, beyond which I could see the vague shape of an opening and the slight giveaway trail of the old man's declared previous visit. I wished I had worn my chaps, but too late then. I pushed forward, cursed as the thorns tore at my shirt and wrists, but I finally forced my way in through to the entrance and lit the lamp.

The interior of the cave smelled of the dead, or was that the influence of the old goat's words. Either way, the dusty dank smell combined with the whistling noise that pervaded the interior was not overly pleasant. The whistling was the result of a chimney rock, a hollow above the cave through which the breeze at the entrance exited back to the sky whence it had come. No spirits, simply the wind. That reassuring thought quickly vanished as I made my way deeper into the cave. There was rustling, and I guess rats or maybe a rattler was disturbed enough to move, but not to sound off. I unhooked the hammer strap of the Colt just in case it was a snake.

Slowly my eyes became accustomed to the gloom and by the flickering light from the lantern I surveyed what was left of the men who had undoubtedly accompanied the gold headed for Dallas, the troops assigned to oversee the reformation of a post-war Lone Star State of Texas. Their bones were littered the visible length of the cave, remnants of ragged blue clinging to white bones, some intact head to toe and others scattered by animals. Everyone wore ragged Union Army blue and two had the faded chevrons on their sleeves of a corporal and a top sergeant. I counted nine skulls, several with obvious bullet wounds and others simply bashed in before or after they had been shot; there was no way of telling. There was an array of Trapdoor Springfield carbines stacked in tipi fashion free from rust in the dry interior, and the two non-coms each carried a holstered Colt .45 Thumb-buster, both of which were unfired with fully charged and capped cylinders. The sergeant, whose body was mummified, it being situated directly beneath the chimney, had a Remington revolver in his waxen, skinned, bony hand. It was empty of shot and each cap had been detonated. He stared up at me, the empty eye sockets leaking dust. But there was no sign of the major supposedly commanding this small dead unit of the 6th Cavalry.

I looked around in my detective way and imagined the scene as it probably went down. The cave filled with snoring sleeping troopers, the gold in large bank bags (strong boxes would have been too heavy for the mule train over that rough hillside terrain), their rifles piled like tipis by the entrance, unsuspecting, happy to be inside and out of the weather for a night. Then the major and the sergeant quickly walking amongst the sleeping men, shooting as they went. Perhaps the major turning to his top sergeant, maybe speaking, maybe not; words wasted in the echoing thunder of the guns discharged in such a confined space, then capping him as he turned to face him. I wondered at the coldness of such an act of violence, but only briefly. I had learned long ago never to be surprised by the cruelty of mankind and gave little quarter to my enemies, knowing full well what little quarter they would give me. For a brief moment, Wildcat and Annie Blue crossed my mind and lingered for a moment, just long enough for me to ask myself what I was doing so far from Peaceful.

But I had not come to mourn the dead. I moved among them again and again, finding little more of interest. I was about to make my way back to the entrance when my toe hooked a leather strap, half covered by sand and debris, at the end of which was a heavy canvas and leather bag. The canvas was in good order, but the leather was dry and cracked. Kneeling, I tore the top around the securing brass lock and shook the contents into the dust. Double eagles. I counted fifty gold coins, one thousand dollars, a tiny fraction of the missing gold. Salvaging a more substantial but smaller empty canvas shoulder bag from the body of one of the troopers, I placed the coins inside, straightened and made my way back to the entrance. I turned once, looking back toward the dead soldiers, young men who had found the big darkness, had done their duty and died for a long-dead nothing cause Texas would have survived and prospered, gold or no gold. That was the Texas way.

Hector was sitting by a small smokeless fire brewing coffee as I emerged blinking into the bright sunlight. With the smell of the coffee and the clean fresh air filling my lungs, I suddenly realized how shallow my breathing had been whilst in the cave. I made my way over to the Morgan and deposited the leather bag and the two loaded handguns I had retrieved in to my saddlebag.

The old man watched me carefully.

'Find what you were looking for, Santana?'

'Some of it, enough to pay my wages, but for the most part I guess it is long gone, along with the person who killed those men, and it is not likely we will find either.'

'Case closed then, is it?'

'No, sir,' I said, 'not until I have the bastard who was behind Kathleen Riley's killer under my gun.'

That answer seemed to please him. 'You want some coffee?'

★ ★ ★

I stayed with the old man that evening and night, in no hurry to get back to Dry Water. It was true what I had told him, the bulk of the gold was gone along with the officer who had killed them. Odd coins would no doubt turn up but the Holy Grail that was the Mother Lode, along with the major, was long gone.

How wrong can a smart man be?

The morning I departed, I believe Hector and I were on good terms. He accompanied me down to the cleft in the rocks where we had first met and he

150

handed me a jug of what he reckoned to be his finest 'shine and gave the dog a final petting. We left him there, me with the promise that if there were any further developments I would get word back to him and him wishing me Godspeed in a language I did not understand, but got the gist of anyway.

12

A Short Ride to Purgatory

The sun was high in a clear blue Texas sky when I finally walked the Morgan along Dry Water's deserted Main Street. I gave the stable lad the usual instructions regarding the mare's needs, along with four bits for his troubles. I chatted to him a while then slipped my carbine out of the boot and, shouldering the canvas bag, made my way directly to the Tavern and a relieved-looking Redmond O'Bannion.

'Jesus, son, I thought you were dead for sure. You find what you were looking for up there at Hector's place?'

That was the second time I had been asked that, so I gave the big Irishman the same answer and a brief description of what I had found up there on the mountain.

'You will be moving on now, I guess?'

'No, Red, I'm going to stick around a while. It still troubles me that someone around here was so concerned that Kathleen had uncovered a story about the gold as to warrant her death. That is one big step to take; killing a newspaperman is one thing, but to pay to have a woman shot down in broad daylight is something else. It may just be I am missing something here.'

'It could be, it could well be. Have you taken supper yet?'

'No, I was intending to drop by the Frog. Care to join me?' He nodded and signalled to Jerry he was leaving. It pleased me, as I did not want to be alone that evening — dark thoughts were already creeping into my head. I am not known for my patience, but caution was everything if I did not want to take a hit from an assassin's bullet fired from some dark alley. One thing was for sure, apart from O'Bannion I was very much alone and far from any San Antonio backup.

Later in my room with a fifth of whiskey, the dog at my feet and my eyes once again fixed on the ceiling, I studied on events and wondered if I had been too hasty to write off the Yankee gold. If there was more information to discover, it would have to come to me as I had no idea as to which direction to search for it. Maybe if I hung around a bit, asked questions that would have no answers, at least that might stir up more than a little interest in my comings and goings. That was it then; loafing, exploring the terrain and being overly inquisitive might just draw something or someone out of the shadows. I decided to give it a week and if nothing happened I would report back to Pinkerton, hand in half of the gold I had found — I felt a finder's fee to be in order — and catch the train north for Wyoming. But before that I intended, if all else failed, to use some of the coins as seed money.

I did not have to wait the full week.

Elmore Cream was a big man. He was just as O'Bannion had described him when I first arrived in Dry Water and he was giving me the lowdown on Danny Doyle, his one-time travelling companion. A large man dressed overall in black pants, shirt and jacket, topped off with a black duster that almost reached to the ground. He was standing in the open double doorway of the livery stable when Bart and I rode in from a trip out into the foothills east of Dry Water. The dog took one look at the dark figure and bellied down behind a water tank. I guessed he had run into the big man before with a none-too-happy doggy outcome.

'The mutt yours?' The voice hoarse, pitched low, the words softly spoken.

I had been asked that tiresome question so many times and had replied with a variety of answers, so I just nodded.

'He's got more lives than a cat, that one.'

'What can I do for you, sir?' I asked. 'I assume you were waiting for me?'

'You assume right, Mr Santana, or are you really the Peaceful River Kid?'

I smiled, 'What can I do for you, sir?'

'Cream, Elmore Cream, and it's more what I can do for you.'

'Oh, and that would be?'

'Mr Doyle would like you to drop by his ranch for lunch tomorrow. Purgatory, just south of the Creek. But you know that, you've been sniffing around there enough.'

'And just why would Mr Doyle want to see me?'

'One of the hands told him you were looking for a homestead out that way. He has no problem with that, but he would like to talk to you, him and you maybe being neighbours and all.'

Cream did not sound like a man who actually believed what he was saying, and there was just the faintest hint of a smile around his wide, thin-lipped mouth.

'I would be happy to join him for lunch. Would dress be formal or casual?'

Now I was smiling, letting him see I was not in any way fooled by the warm invitation.

'Whatever, there will be someone to meet you at the main gate. Shall we say around noon?'

'We could say that, Elmore. OK if I call you Elmore?'

He did not answer, simply turned on his heel, walked across to the corral and easily heaved his heavy weight up onto the saddle of the large black tied there. His job done, the message delivered.

★   ★   ★

I spent the evening jawing and drinking with O'Bannion before turning in for an early night. I needed a good night's sleep. My troubled thoughts had led me down dark roads to dreams I would sooner not have had. A cave filled with soldiers being slaughtered by their commanding officer, their long dead souls trapped in a dusty cave, howling at the wind and their forlorn cries echoed by coyotes, the sound racing up the chimney rock alerting the whole of the mountain that they were trapped, dead and demanding justice for their brutal passing. There are no bugles, no drums, no Taps, only the wind.

★   ★   ★

I dressed in the black Stetson and a black town suit I borrowed from O'Bannion's store on the understanding that if I got any blood or bullet holes in any of it, I would pay the full price. But if I returned it in one piece, I could have my deposit back and the outfit could be returned to the rack. I strapped on the rig and Colt once owned by James J. Watson of Baltimore rather than my own, just to see if there was any reaction to my having it. I left the Morgan with Bart and the kid, and took the trail out to Purgatory on a hired roan with an easy gait; the horse, the boy had assured me, had a mild temperament. The journey took the best part of forty minutes, riding at a leisurely pace, not wanting to get too much of Texas on the suit or the discomfort of wearing my grey duster on such a warm sunny morning.

Just as Cream had told me, there was a guard stationed at the wooden gate, over which Doyle's pitchfork brand, gleaming in polished steel, was suspended from a frame of stripped Ponderosa pine. I reined the roan in and waited as the young man approached me, a sheet of paper in one hand and a shotgun at the trail in the other. 'Can I help you, sir?' he said.

'I'm here by invitation of Mr Doyle.'

'Your name, sir?'

I wondered if this was a regular occurrence or one simply put on for my benefit. 'The Peaceful River Kid,' I said.

He consulted the paper and looked at me, confusion in his young face. Obviously that was not the anticipated reply. 'Are you sure, sir?'

'Am I sure I know my own name?'

'I don't have you on my list is all.'

'Try Lucas Santana then.'

He consulted his list again and looked up at me with relief in his nervous smile.

'That's OK then, Mr Santana. I just need you to leave your sidearm here with me, you can pick it up on the way out.'

'No way, boy. The only way you get my handgun is if you rip it from my cold dead hand.'

I liked the sound of that, something that might catch on one day. I also liked the look of dismay on the youngster's face. He stared up at me, licked his lips, confused, and glanced off toward the small stand of willows dribbling into a trickling stream. Then relief as Elmore Cream rode the big black out the trees, crossed the water and reined in beside him.

'What seems to be the trouble, Billy?'

'Mr Santana is on the list, but he will not give up his firearm, sir.'

'That right, Mr Santana?'

I nodded.

He smiled. 'You planning on shooting

160

anyone this day, Mr Santana?'

'No, it's just a matter of principle, Elmore. Call it a habit if you will, but it's one that has served me well.'

'So the sheriff told me.'

'Deputy sheriff,' I said. 'He is just a county deputy, like it or not.'

'Yes indeed, he told me you said that as well.' Still smiling, he turned to the youngster. 'Let him through, Billy. I think we can handle him up at the house. If he gets a bit rambunctious, I'll call you and you come running. He's a wild one is the Peaceful River Kid.' The smile turned to laughter and we rode side by side up to the big white adobe and timber-framed ranch house that was the headquarters of Purgatory and home of Danny Doyle.

We gave the reins of our horses to a waiting Mexican, who led the animals over to the water trough and then into the shade of the large double-doored stable.

Doyle met us at the door. He stood on the veranda towering over us, an outsized man in every way, except for his voice which was soft, gently British not broad Irish as I had imagined it would be, precise, with each word carefully selected. He was a very fat man, dressed in a pristine white suit with a cream-coloured Panama straw atop his undersized head, red-faced, almost breathless. He stepped down and offered me his chubby damp hand. I took it, a firm handshake something easy to fake, a reassuring welcome, the smile of a grizzly before it bites your head off.

'Welcome to Purgatory, Mr Santana,' he chuckled. 'I never get tired of saying that, sir, and I never will. Come, let's get out of this damned sun and around some cool refreshments.'

We followed him in through the thick wooden doorway, crossed a large hallway and into a living room the like of which I had never seen before. The walls were draped with long guns of every variety, all pristine and polished. In concert with the guns, were the mounted heads of every conceivable animal from

Texas and far beyond — buffalo, elk, moose, cougar, mountain goat, white-tailed deer, wild boar, sometimes more than one of each, a deer with a large rack and a smaller antlered animal beside it. Doyle followed my gaze and asked, 'Do you hunt, Mr Santana?'

'I only ever kill what I need to eat, never for the fun of killing. Never understood the need for that.'

'Whiskey with ice, it's a good Irish. I understand you have a penchant for fine Irish.'

I ignored the remark and took the glass he offered me, clear white ice speckled with the lovely tan colour of the whiskey. He did not offer Cream a drink and the man moved to a quiet corner of the room beside a large oak desk in the centre of which was a bleached white human skull with a neat round hole between the eye sockets. Like the skull, he seemed to watch our every move.

'*Sláinte*,' I said, raising my glass.

'To the old country then, *sláinte* to you, sir.'

I raised my glass and half turned toward the big buffalo, raised it a little higher and sipped the smooth cool alcohol. 'You kill them for their heads or for food?' I asked, genuinely curious.

'Well, let us say I killed them for food although we both know that would not be true. I like to hunt, most Texans do, and these days I consider myself to be of Texas.'

'And him?' I nodded in the direction of the bleached skull. 'Alas, is that poor Yorick?'

He laughed a big belly laugh. 'Are you familiar with *Hamlet*, Mr Santana?'

'I'm well-read, Mr Doyle.'

'Indeed you are, sir, but alas no, that is not poor Yorick, not Mr Shakespeare's court jester. That is the late Major J.P. Hollander, the very, very late Major J.P. Hollander, of the Union Army's 6th Cavalry.'

'You eat the rest of him?' I asked.

Again, that belly laugh. 'No, sir, he went back from whence he came. I had him buried in a shallow grave on a

164

faraway sandbank of Dry Water Creek, close by to where I found him.'

'Found him?'

'Yes, or rather what was left of him, mostly bones and rags washed clear by the rain I suspect, but enough to identify him.'

'You notify the army?'

'What would be the point of that, sir? He was a long time dead and long ago mourned. Best to let sleeping dogs lie, what do you think, Mr Santana?'

'I don't know much about dogs, Mr Doyle, but I do know folk like to know what happened to their loved ones.'

'I don't believe he would have been dearly loved, sir. In fact, I think he would have been reviled for killing the nine men under his command and stealing three quarters of a million dollars of Union Army gold coin.'

'He did that?'

'Oh come, sir, you know very well what I am talking about. We found several double eagles along with the body and you, sir, are looking for that gold now. And the question is, have you found it?'

'The answer to that is I have no idea what you are talking about, Mr Doyle.'

'Very well, let us just assume for one moment that to be true, and as you are not looking for it you will not have found it. I am looking for it and I have not found it either, which means it is still out there to be found. Are you following me thus far, sir?'

I sipped my drink and did not reply.

'Of course you are. I have done some background checking on you; you are a man who hunts for things and often finds them, men mostly. Do you eat them when you find them, Mr Santana?'

Again, I ignored his question.

'Come look at the late major and tell me what you see. Humour a fat old man.' He walked over to the desk and Cream stepped well back from it, never once taking his eyes off me. It was a little unnerving. 'What do you see, Mr Santana?'

I looked closely at the skull. There was the neat round hole — an entrance wound, but no corresponding exit wound.

'Well?' he asked, rubbing his hands together and casting a glance toward Cream.

'Looks to be a low velocity round, bit too big for a .22, maybe a .41. No exit wound so that would make it likely fired close up, but not a contact wound. Someone who knew him maybe, someone he got too close to.'

'Let us assume then whoever did for the good major has the gold.'

'You can assume that I suppose, but if what you say is correct then all you have to do is solve a twenty-year-old murder. Shouldn't be too difficult for a man who can creep up on a big old buff like that one on the wall and kill him.'

Doyle laughed, put his arm around my shoulder, led me back across the room and refilled my glass. 'Do you know what I believe, Mr Santana? I believe you are close to solving that murder and that is what brought you to Dry Water. And it is also why someone took a shot at you in Dry Water and killed the unfortunate Kathleen Riley who, I assure you, I held in high regard. And had you not been so rash as to kill him, then we might be a lot closer than we are.'

'We?'

'Yes, we. I suggest we join forces and share the proceeds upon completion and you give up this silly pretence of wanting to be a homesteader. What do you say to that, Mr Santana?'

'Honestly?'

'Yes, sir, honestly.'

'I think you are crazy, Mr Doyle, a crazy man with gold fever.'

The fat man's demeanour changed instantly. His face reddened, he snorted moisture from his nose and nodded toward Cream, prearranged I supposed. Cream was quick, but nowhere near as fast as me. His Colt was only halfway out of the leather when mine was clear, cocked and the muzzle pointed straight at Doyle's fat belly. Both men froze. I moved and set my back firmly against the wall. I didn't want anyone behind me and it was certain the two men were not alone.

'Elmore,' I said quietly, 'you shuck that rig and the hideaway you have in your right boot.' He unbuckled the heavy gunbelt and let it fall to the floor, then bent down and gently withdrew a Derringer from his right boot and tossed it aside, a puzzled look on his pale face. 'I've been around, Elmore, don't sweat it. Now outside, both of you. Elmore, you get my horse walked out and one for Mr Doyle here. He is going to accompany me to young Billy and beyond. I see you or anyone else on our tail, your boss will lose an ear. You got that, Elmore Cream?'

'Mr Doyle does not ride.' The words were softly spoken, but there was a fire in his dark eyes.

'No problem, get him a buggy. The Mex can drive, but get it done.'

'I'll remember this, Santana.' Cream

snarled the words at me.

'I'm counting on that, Elmore. I want you to remember it and remember it well; next time you come at me will be your last.' I prodded Doyle out of the door and waited. The man was sweating from every pore. His eyes burned in to me like hot irons; I have never seen such hatred.

It took a while, but eventually the buggy arrived with the roan tied to the boot. I told Cream to go belly-down on the veranda and stay there while I prodded the fat man into the buggy beside the Mexican wrangler and mounted the roan. At one point a half-dressed man rushed out of what I assumed to be the bunkhouse with a six in his hand. I did not hesitate, and put a round in his stockinged left foot. He screamed in pain and ducked back into the building that he had only left seconds before. Such is life. Young Billy was not on gate duty so, as I had guessed, that was all a bit of a show for my benefit. Five miles down the road, certain we were not being followed, I told the Mex to take Doyle home.

The fat man had not said a single word on the journey, but recovered some of his composure knowing he was about to be released. 'Not the way I thought the day would go down, sir, no not at all, but we will meet again I am sure. And maybe given more time I can persuade you that my way is the best way for both of us. Oh,' he smiled and added reassuringly, 'do not fret about friend Elmore Cream. He has a violent temper 'tis true, but I will ensure he does not bother you in any way. Wouldn't want to hinder you in your search now, would we?'

The hint of a returning belly laugh, a feeling the fat man knew more than he was letting on. And then they were gone and I turned the roan's head back toward Dry Water.

13

The Old Family Bible

I had not been back in Dry Water long before O'Bannion sought me out at his wife's café. I was sitting alone in my preferred chair with my back to the wall and a clear view of the door. I was already on my second coffee refill.

He dragged a chair out in front of me without being invited and sat there, perched on the edge of the chair staring at me, waiting, eventually saying a long drawn out 'Well . . . ?'

'Well, nothing very much. I did not learn a lot other that the fact that they do not like me. Can you believe that?'

'No way. You are such a likeable fellow. They just don't cotton to Yankees around here still.' He grinned. 'But what else?'

'Well, one thing Doyle did make clear

is that he is also looking for the gold, as we thought, but he has no idea where to start looking. I guess he has played out the caves and workings around Purgatory. He is a worried man. He believes he is close enough to smell it, but not close enough to touch it.'

'You think it is there?'

'No.'

'Anything about Kathleen?'

'Again, no. Nothing other than the fact that he says the killer Watson was after me, which we both know to be a lie, and there seems to be only one reason to lie about that.'

'And that is?'

'He knows the truth of it, as do I.'

*　*　*

The next few days passed quietly and the fine early autumn weather held fast, geese filled the skies daily and the white tail deer were in the rut. The pines would hold their green but the aspens, the willow and the live oak changed

173

dramatically, their colours glowing on the nearby hillside and as they shed their leaves, their branches draped with resting migratory birds. The ever-vigilant raptors could once again clearly see their winter prey and took of them liberally. Texas, nature in the raw, critters sometimes often more violent that their human counter-parts, and it was that violence that haunted me as I sat in the chair and smoked my first smoke of the day, wondering about the dead and why I had not given up cigarettes as I had promised myself earlier. I spent several of the double eagles I had found in the cave around town. One got me some change from Doyle's bank, another in the cantina — that one raised a few eyebrows — and one in paying part of my hotel bill with enough to hold the room for another two weeks. The desk clerk examined the coin, but said nothing. I wondered how soon before he or Harry Ballinger the bank manager would get the word out to Doyle. There were no Purgatory visitors to the town and

O'Bannion complained, jokingly I think, that I was bad for business; and the dog always at my heel was also a pain in the ass.

The deputy Max Hadley had on several occasions crossed the street to avoid me, and on each occasion I stood there with my jacket open and my thumbs hooked in my gunbelt, but he had not taken the bait, and a fish that will not feed is not worthy of my thoughts, which were constantly returning to the dead soldiers in Hector Dulles' cave. I owed them, or at least someone did, and I was there to pick up their tab. I tried to explain this to O'Bannion. The Irishman nodded sagely but made no comment. I asked him to put me a small bag of supplies together, including a bottle and some pipe tobacco, along with a couple of empty gunny sacks. I explained that I would be gone for a few days. His only comment to that was that he would be glad to see the back of me for a while, and that I was to be sure and take the damned dog along with me.

★ ★ ★

A little after noon Hector Dulles met me at the cleft in the rocks and, recognizing Bart who had run ahead of me rather than his usual subservient position at my heel, lowered the Springfield as he stepped clear of cover.

'Thought it was maybe you.'

He knelt and ruffled Bart's neck and the animal rolled onto its, back baring its stomach to him — something a dog like Bart would rarely do.

'Am I welcome?' I asked, reining in the Morgan.

'The dog is, so I guess I'll have to put up with you as well. You plan on staying long?'

'A couple of nights maybe, if you are easy with that.'

'Sure, why not, gets kinda lonely up here sometimes. Put your horse in the corral and your trappings on the bunk. Make yourself at home. I've got to tend the still for a while, but I will be back down before nightfall.'

'Is it all right if I use your lanterns?'

'Sure enough. You going back into that damned cave?' He didn't wait for an answer but, shaking his head, he turned and set off up the hill to where his mule was grazing.

* * *

There was little more than a hint of a breeze on that hillside and still the chimney rock moaned, and I wondered had it always been so or was it the presence of the nine dead soldiers that called the wind down in to the cave. I set the lanterns up on each side of the cavern and slowly and methodically went through the pockets and shoulder bags of each of the skeletons. The few that were spread around, their bones mixed with those of their dead companions, were difficult to search, but the six whole bodies were quickly dealt with and within an hour I had a gunny sack filled with the identifiable remains of the dead. Watches, faded letters and photographs of loved ones, some coins and bank notes; here and there I had found a medal inscribed with the name of the recipient, and even a Wells Fargo bank book showing the soldier had $75 in a Memphis bank account.

And then there were the crude handmade dog tags, a practice not officially adopted until long after the Civil War. Prior to that, young men about to die were worried they would be lost and forgotten, as thousands of their fellow soldiers of both blue and the grey were. Names carved on wooden discs, soft metal circles, even on the reverse of their belt buckles. I found them all, the nine names of the dead warriors of the 6th Cavalry. I also collected over 200 rounds of .45-70 ammo and one of the best of the Springfield Trapdoors: the former to resupply Dulles and the latter for spare parts should his rifle ever fail him.

* * *

After a fine supper of venison stew, carrots and potatoes, I broke out the bottle of whiskey and the pouch of tobacco O'Bannion had packed for me and I was pleased with the old man's genuine delight. The stove was open and glowing. Bart was stationed in front of it and I had that very mellow and relaxed feeling that goes with warmth, whiskey and a well-fed belly.

'How long have you lived in this place?' I asked him, wanting to break the silence before I dozed off.

'On this mountain? Maybe fifty years. Lived further down but when I hurt my back in a fall I decided to move closer to the still and that's when I found this place. It was run down some, had been empty for a long while, but I evicted the wildlife and fixed the place up good. Been here fifteen years and some now.'

'Who lived here before?'

'Middle-aged couple, Myrtle and Henry Adams, used to see them occasionally when I was on the mountain. He was a miner. I hear he struck it rich up in

Llano, the North Texas Hill Country, and moved on to San Antonio. That was maybe three years or so before I moved in.'

'So, they lived hereabouts when the killings took place?'

'Don't rightly know. I guess not though, else they would have alerted the local law. Not easy for soldiers and pack mules to go unnoticed around here.'

'Maybe,' I said quietly, 'and then again maybe not.'

He thought about that for a very long moment, stoked his pipe and refilled our glasses. He put his to his lips, then looked over the rim at me, looked me straight in the eye. 'You thinking what I'm thinking, Santana?'

'Could well be, Hector, could well be.'

'I'll be damned.'

'Do you know what happened to them in San Antonio?'

'No idea. I guess if what you are thinking is right, then they probably lived the good life on top of the hill and maybe they still do.'

'They leave anything around, old letters, anything like that?'

'I cleared all of their stuff out, good stuff at that, like they left in a hurry and travelled light. Burned most of it. All I kept was an old family bible. It didn't seem right to burn that.'

'Do you still have it?'

'In a trunk up at the still. I'll bring it down tomorrow if'n the mice haven't eaten it.'

★　★　★

I spent most of the next day on my own sorting through the bits and pieces I had gathered in the cave, Bart having chosen to go along with Hector to the still. I wondered if Billy Roy Stone's 75 dollars were still in the Memphis bank or if John T. Roberts' daughter had grown to be as lovely as the young mother in the faded Daguerreotype holding her close? And what were the histories the other young uniformed men accompanying Top Sergeant Andy Cole, the non-com I suspected of having taken part in the slaughter? Nine men, nine stories all scattered and collected, to be delivered in a gunny sack to the Pinkerton Agency in San Antonio, where I was certain Joshua Beaufort, being an ex-army man himself, would ensure the relatives of the dead men would be tracked down and a closure of sorts reached after nearly two decades.

Hector Dulles arrived home just before sunset preceded by an eager Bart who brushed against me; he seemed either pleased or relieved or maybe both that I was still there.

The large leather-bound family bible Hector dumped out of a canvas bag and on to the table had an old dry smell to it, and the gold leaf on the cover had long since dulled. I opened it carefully hoping that the family records would be there, as was the custom with such books, and clearly readable. They were, a family record of births, marriages and deaths clearly annotated in various hands, but the only thing of any real interest to me was that it recorded Myrtle's family and not that of the Adams family, which I was expecting it to be. Her maiden name was Grant and she had married Henry Adams in 1861, the very year the Rebs had fired on Fort Sumter. After making a few notes, I carefully returned the heavy book to its canvas bag and sat back in my chair.

'Any help to you?' Hector asked.

'Could be,' I said. 'You want to keep it or can I take it back down with me?'

'You keep it, I got no need for a bible up here. I see God every day and never more so than this time of the year. You a God-fearing man, Santana?'

'I'm not sure there is a God, at least as you see him. I figure if there was, would he let a man like me loose on the streets, or Doyle, or the man who wiped out that patrol, and certainly not the man who gunned down Kathleen Riley.'

He thought about that for a moment and asked, 'You ever figure you might just be his instrument to putting those great wrongs to rights?'

It was a thought, but not one I would dwell upon. It was hard to imagine me as an instrument of the Lord. Changing the subject, I looked at the dog curled up at his feet, his chin resting on one of the old man's worn down work boots.

'You can keep the dog if you want,' I said.

'Is he yours to give away?'

'Point taken.' He was right of course.

'In any case, it wouldn't be fair on him. I had a dog up here one time. Some crazy hunter shot it. They make good targets. I buried him along with the fool who shot him, buried him deep in a clearing just beyond the bluff, buried the dog on top of him.'

'You killed the man who shot your dog?'

'Wouldn't you?' He asked the question with trace of a smile on his lips, knowing, I suspect, what the answer to that would be were I to give him one. I thought about my threat to the deputy, but did not answer the old man's question and I do not believe he really expected me to.

★ ★ ★

I left early next morning and Hector rode with me to the cleft in the rocks, gave the dog a final hug and waved at my back.

'See you again soon I hope, Santana.'

I raised my hand in acknowledgement, but did not turn around. I liked Hector Dulles and could clearly see why Kathleen had enjoyed the old man's company.

★ ★ ★

That evening, after a brief word with O'Bannion and supper at the Frog, I retired to the hotel lobby, scrounged pen, ink, paper and envelope from the disgruntled clerk and wrote a detailed report to Joshua Beaufort, asking for him to check on the possible whereabouts of

185

Myrtle and Henry Adams — adding that if they were not to found under that name, her maiden name Grant would be worth a look-see. I mailed the letter the next morning and waited for a reply. The Pinkerton Agency was good at finding people who wished to remain lost and they would eventually even have Jesse James in custody. This hunt took them the best part of a week, a week of my kicking my heels, playing chequers with O'Bannion and the occasional foray out to the foothills, wanting to be seen about, hoping Doyle or Cream would break cover and give me something to shoot at. I am really mean when bored and I did not doubt for one moment that Doyle had given the OK for the hit on Kathleen Riley.

The letter was on Pinkerton headed paper with the wide open-eyed trademark, brief and to the point. Beaufort or one of the agents had tracked down a widowed woman by the name of Myrtle Grant residing in an old people's rest home in the suburbs of San Antonio, not far from the old Alamo Mission. She fitted the age group perfectly. The letter asked how did I want to proceed? To save time I wired back, not wanting anyone else to interview her, making that clear and saying that I would be there in two days. I packed my gear, re-hired the suit from O'Bannion, caught the same departed Overland as had brought in the letter, but had to chase it hard on the hired roan to the Del Moro swing station. It was a long bouncing journey with one overnighter at Florisville, forty miles south of the city.

Jacob Benbow met me at the Overland office with a warm handshake and a welcoming smile. A tall young man, lanky and very reliable, a one-time partner of Beaufort. Apparently, Jesse's fellow outlaw Bob Ford had done the dirty on his friend and shot him in the back, thus freeing Benbow to work with me if needed. I was pleased to see him; it had been a long time passing. He had me registered at the Union Hotel and once done, we shared a drink in the hotel bar and I brought him up to date on my thoughts regarding the missing gold.

★ ★ ★

The Serendipity Retirement Home for Ladies was a large white building, set back and secluded from the main road by an ivy-covered and rose-draped wall, high enough to keep young people out and to keep the old folk in. The nurse, a tall, pale-faced, elegant middle-aged woman, welcomed me, shook my hand and invited me into her pristine yet Spartan office. A crucifix on the wall, a mahogany desk and various illustrations from biblical events depicted in oil paint on the walls. She slid across the room, her feet completely hidden by the long grey skirt, which brushed the floor in front and behind her.

'Please take a seat, Mr Santana.' She indicated the chair in front of her desk. 'My name is Sister Reardon and I have this day spoken with Mr Pinkerton, who advised me that this visit is to seek out the background to events Mrs Grant may have witnessed many years ago.'

I nodded.

'I have asked her if she is happy to sit and speak with you and she is quite happy to do so. However, I must warn you that she can be a little distant and confused. You must take that into account, no matter what she might tell you. For instance, she believes her husband is still alive and with her. In fact he has been dead for five years now.'

'How long has she been resident here?' I asked.

'Six years to be exact. Henry brought her to us when she first became unwell and donated a considerable amount of money to our foundation in order to ensure she remains and is happy here for the rest of her natural life.'

'How unwell?'

'That will be for you to decide, but I assure you she is in the best of health physically.'

'How much money?' I asked.

She smiled at me over the top of her wire-framed spectacles, 'I am sorry, sir, I am not at liberty to speak of such matters, but it is true her husband was extremely wealthy, a gold miner I believe, and a shrewd businessman who did not squander that which God put his way, but rather invested it in folk less fortunate than himself and those who would benefit most from his good fortune. He has donated considerable amounts of money to foundations and enterprises such as ours across Texas and is responsible for the building of at least three churches, one of which is right here in San Antonio.'

I nodded again. 'Thank you, Sister.'

'You are welcome. Any friend of Allan's is a friend of ours. Come, I will take you to her.' She stood up and I followed her from the office.

The room was medium-sized and compact, tastefully decorated and minimally furnished. Two comfortable looking cushioned armchairs, a dining table, a small bureau, a single bed beneath a large picture window that faced out onto an attractive flower garden. There was also a third armchair, a large leather very masculine affair set in one corner of the room next to a small coffee table.

'This is Mr Santana, your gentleman caller for the day, Mrs Grant. The gentleman from Wyoming I was telling you about this morning.'

Myrtle Grant was old, frail of body, pink of cheek and grey of hair. She also had the clearest pale blue eyes I have ever seen. Mirrors or windows I was not sure, but as she looked up from the book she had been reading and closed it, I felt her intent gaze going far beyond my face and into a dark somewhere I rarely ventured. After seemingly satisfied with what she saw there, she smiled at me, got to her feet and offered me her hand. She held my hand tightly in hers and looked beyond me to Sister Reardon and said, 'Henry will be joining us, Sister Reardon?'

'I'm certain he will, Mrs Grant. He is

never far away.' She smiled fondly at the old lady, nodded her head to me and floated from the room, closing the door quietly behind her.

Myrtle looked to the left and the right of her, then behind her, before turning back to me, lowering her voice, almost whispering as if she was sharing a secret never to be told. 'Henry and I have been expecting you for a very long time, Mr Santana of Wyoming.' She turned her head toward the large empty leather chair on the far side of the room. 'We have been expecting this young man for a long time haven't we, Henry, a very long time.'

It took a long while for Myrtle Grant to get the story in sequence, her words spoken softly and often broken mid-sentence by long pauses, misty-eyed, looking beyond me to the leather armchair as if to get affirmation of her words. I listened carefully, nodding encouragingly at her account of one storm-blasted, tornado-driven night up by Indian Rock in South Texas.

14

A Cold Night on a Dark Mountain

'It was always the weather up there on that mountain, I recall it so well. Its many changes were not to be feared, Mr Santana. It was God's country and He was at hand. He was my right arm, my strength, both then and as He is now.

'Early that morning, the sun was hidden in a grey mist. The deer, usually so quiet and friendly around the cabin, were fidgety, moving swiftly from one grass patch to another, never settling to graze, their heads always up, alert, seemingly distracted by the dark blue and black cumulonimbus clouds gathering on the higher ground and already hiding the distant mountain tops. The air was very still, tainted with a curious smell of burning sulphur.'

Her conspiratorial tone was somehow heightened by her half-closed eyes as she gazed fixedly into some middle distance, a place I could not see but could feel.

'Gradually the mist vanished, replaced by the low-lying thunder clouds then, quite suddenly and without warning, the sky was alive with lightning, the yellow fingers lancing from out of the darkness above our cabin. The deer fled and a fork of yellow struck a nearby live oak, draping the branches with fire and smoke, the flames both at one and the same time fanned by the rising wind and doused by the sudden sheeting of rain.'

I closed my eyes, the sound of her voice soothing, but fired by an inner passion. I could see Hector's cabin, see the flashing fire, smell the storm and hear the rolling of the thunder.

'You are not sleeping, sir?' she asked.

'No,' I said, opening my eyes and smiling, 'I am picturing the night. Your voice is most compelling.'

'Henry and I,' she continued, 'stood

side by side, staring out at the tempest-ravaged clearing. I was praying and Henry's strong arms around me gave me hope and a promise of a protection I knew he could not be sure of delivering. The elements hold sway over man and beast, Mr Santana. We were at His mercy. We stood like that, locked together, watching as the man and the mule train appeared as ghostly apparitions from out of the rainswept, lightning-fired darkness. He drove the frightened heavily-laden animals into the pole corral and, fighting his flapping slicker, made his way to the cabin door just as Henry threw it open, holding it hard against the wind, and together they fought to get the heavy door closed and bolted hard against the pounding storm.'

Myrtle paused and removed her glasses, wiping them with a silk handkerchief as if her pale blue eyes were the fountain of her gathered memories. I waited.

'He almost fell into the cabin. He was a big man, I think a major, in the blue uniform of the Union Army. Stripped of his long coat, his clothes fitted him like a glove, a muscular body. The wet white shirt rather than the regulation blue clinging to his chest was blood-spattered, as were his neck and bare forearms, the blood running with the rain and dripping onto our cabin floor. He was unshaven, and there was a madness in his wild eyes, a look of genuine fear, panic, as if he had been pursued by the hounds of Hell rather than a freak late summer thunderstorm. He turned toward the window trembling, staring out into the yard as if expecting some spectral figure to follow him out of the darkness. He did not speak or in any way react to our presence in the room. Standing there breathing heavily, he was parade-ground erect.'

There was a long pause and Myrtle fixed her pale eyes on the empty leather chair. I wondered if I should move or stay, speak or remain silent. I had read somewhere that you should never awaken a sleepwalker and I was reluctant to interrupt her reverie.

Myrtle broke the long silence, her gaze still fixed to the empty chair. ''You are hurt, sir. Come sit down. I will tend to your wound,' I said. He stared at me as if seeing me for the first time.'

Her voice suddenly dropped, became harsh, gritty. ''*A mountain witch? Keep away from me, witch.*' He snarled the words at me, then repeated them words, shouting, almost screaming them. '*Keep your hands away from me, witch.*'

'Back in those days, Henry was no lightweight and he moved to my side, but before he could speak, the angry man punched him in the mouth and then again on the jaw and my dear Henry went down on to the floor, dead to the world. I was so afraid, more for Henry than myself you understand.

''You crazy bastard!' I screamed the words at him.'

She raised her voice and I could see the whites of her knuckles as she clenched her hands into tiny fists and struggled with the memory of the assault.

'It was the first and only time in my

life I ever used a cuss word and in some ways I was glad Henry did not hear me. I rushed over to Henry, but the big man caught me and tossed me back across the room and against our small bureau as if I were no more than a rag doll. The bureau's single drawer popped open upon the impact, spilling its contents onto the cabin floor.'

Her voice again dropped. ''*Shut your mouth, witch,*' he shouted at me. '*Speak when you are spoken to. How long is this tempest of your making likely to last — an hour, a day, what?*'

'I did not answer, for I could not. Henry groaned, moaned like a wounded animal and tried to get to his feet, but the man drew a pistol and cracked it against the side of his head and again he went down. I dropped to my knees, put my hands together and prayed for our salvation.

''*He won't help you today, witch,*' he said. '*He done left this part of the country early this morning, took nine saints with him. You want to make it eleven,*

you just keep on the way you are going.''
Quite suddenly her speech slowed, calmed.
'Would you like some iced tea, Mr Santana? Henry loves iced tea. I can ring the bell and ask for some if you so wish.'

'No thank you, Mrs Grant, but if you would like me to leave I will not detain you further.' I was lost, out of my depth by a country mile.

'No, of course not. Henry insists that you know and understand. We were not thieves. We took the gold to do God's work and that is what we have done, together, always together.'

'Gold? What gold was this?' I asked, although I already knew.

'He moved towards me, that poor crazy man, and just as he reached me another lightning strike and again the crack of thunder. The lightning danced around the exterior of the cabin, illuminating the corral, the frightened mules baying and crashing against the strong, railed fence. He stopped in his tracks, the fear in his eyes apparent even in the half darkness.

''No more',' he said, not to me but to his own reflection in the thick glass of the window. '*I killed them all, witch. They are out there, I can see them, hear them falling under my gun. That damned private with a pistol in his hand, but not knowing what to do with it, dropping it as my bullet tore into him. Then the damned top sergeant, the crazy sonofabitch, the only other man to react, rolling over from his bedroll, picking up the dropped side-arm and firing five wild rounds at me, clipping me with one then going down as I shot him through the left eye. Oh, no more, witch, I know your game, this storm is your doing.*' They were the last words he ever uttered.

'He turned his attention once more to me. He saw the open drawer and he saw the gun in my hand, but he had no chance to stop it. I shot him dead. The single bullet struck him cleanly between the eyes. It was very strange. I think he was dead before he hit the shaking floor and the thunder roll that followed his fall was almost too perfect. Was it the sound of God calling him or was He chastising me for taking a life?'

She waited for an answer I did not have.

'I do not believe you had any other choice, Mrs Grant. Sometimes it happens that way,' was the best I could think of.

'Have you ever shot anyone, Mr Santana?'

'Yes,' I said.

'More than one?'

'Yes,' I said again.

'Is there any one person more than any other whose life you wished you had not taken?'

I had to think about that. Searching my own soul was not the reason for my visit to the Serendipity Retirement Home, but it needed thinking about and it deserved an answer. 'One man I wished I had not been forced to kill, his name was Darryl Jones from New Orleans. He did not need to die. Circumstances sometimes force a person into an act they would not perform were there time

201

to think or reason.'

She smiled sadly, satisfied with my answer for what it was worth.

'I dropped the little gun Henry had taught me to shoot and moved swiftly to his side, and stayed there close by him for the rest of our lives together. We never shared our secret discovery of the gold-laden mules, never shared the killing of the major and we never spoke of it, not even to each other.

'The following morning, we packed what little we needed and waited as the big blow passed by and drove itself out in the distant valleys. We gathered the mules together and pushed them all of the long journey to Llano in the Texas Hill Country, and on the way we buried Major J.P. Hollander, for that was his name, in a shallow grave on a sandbank of Dry Water Creek, and along with him we buried a handful of the double eagles which, should he ever be found, would confuse any unlikely pursuit. We sprinkled them like breadcrumbs and for several miles we tossed the odd coin into the creek, but we knew one day you would come along and that is all right now, isn't it, Henry.' It was not a question as I would know it and there was no answer from the leather chair.

I waited patiently through a long silence, but there was no more. She smiled sweetly at me, picked up her book and began to read, her lips moving silently from time to time as she struggled, I guessed, with the small print.

I sat there in my own silence, thinking it through. The gold was gone and as far as I could see it had gone to a better cause than the one intended. After a while, just as I had made up my mind to leave, she got to her feet and crossed the room to the small bureau, opened a drawer and took out a little leather pouch and handed it to me. 'Henry tells me it is time to give this away and I am sure he meant it for you, Mr Santana.' She looked over at the armchair, smiled and turned back to me. 'Henry says that yes, he did.'

I took the pouch from her and undid

the drawstring and shook out a little double-barrelled, nickel-plated Remington and four .41 calibre brass cartridges. 'Thank you,' I said and slipped the bag into my coat pocket, but she had already returned her attention to her book and was for that moment lost to me.

'What are you reading?' I asked, reluctant to leave without a farewell.

She looked up and smiled. 'The story of a young boy and the river by Mr Mark Twain, *The Adventures of Huckleberry Finn*. Do you know of it, sir?'

'No but I enjoyed *Tom Sawyer*, so I guess I will get around to it sooner or later.'

'Sooner is always best, Mr Santana. Leave an address with Sister Reardon and I will see to it that when I have finished the book I will send it to you.'

'That is very kind of you, ma'am. I will send you a book in return just as soon as I can, and I thank you for your time, Mrs Grant.'

I picked up my hat, bowed, turned and made for the door, but she called my name and, as I turned to her, said, 'You are not of Texas, sir?'

'No, ma'am, originally I am from Virginia, but now of Wyoming.'

'No matter, we say you are a gentleman. Good luck and goodbye.'

As I reached for the handle, the door opened and Sister Reardon smiled and led the way to the main front door. 'I trust your visit was fruitful and that you have that damned firearm in your pocket.'

'Damned firearm, Sister Reardon?' I could not hide the smile.

'We are not all saints, sir, although we would like to be.'

I gave her my card with the Wyoming address on it. 'Mrs. Grant wants to send me a book; it will find me there. Also, I have a book for her, her old family bible as it happens, and I am sure she would be pleased to have it returned, as she left it someplace a long, long time ago. Someone from the Pinkerton office will drop it by for her with my compliments. Please see that she gets it and knows that it is from me.'

'Surely I will. You are quite taken with her, are you not? I could see that she liked you.'

I touched my hat and smiled at her. 'I'm great with old people, fools, horses and dogs — anyone or anything else, not so much. Myrtle Grant recognized me for the gentleman I am. That does not happen to me very often.'

We shook hands and I left her standing by the wide door. I think both of our lives gained a little from my one brief meeting with Myrtle Adams née Grant.

★ ★ ★

In the bar of my hotel much later that day, Beaufort, Benbow and I concluded that there was little more to be done. The gold was gone, spent, untraceable and far away. Beaufort studied the whiskey in his glass. 'One of those mysteries I guess, it will become a legend. It will be as The Lost Dutchman or *Los Almagres*, Jim Bowie's lost mine, always out there waiting, ever a quest for a bold or foolish someone. Another Holy Grail of gold that will never be found. *Buena Saluda*, my friends. Here's to Myrtle, Henry and nine dead soldiers.'

On that note we emptied our glasses and retired to the dining room and dinner.

But it was far from over.

15

The Big Showdown

There was not a great deal of work to do in the San Antonio field office at that time, so Beaufort suggested that it would be useful to have Jacob Benbow return to Dry Water with me. He could visit the whistling cave of the dead and maybe organize some sort of military service and Christian burial for the troopers there; take the preacher up there, dig some graves, organize a rifle squad and give them a proper resting place, maybe even Taps, find a horn player and send them on their way in style. Headstones and perhaps a masted flag. Did I think the old man Hector would mind? I said no, he would be pleased to help. So that was settled over breakfast and we were on the Overland stage headed back to Dry Water with

Benbow carrying his precious Henry repeating rifle in a buckskin scabbard.

Leaving early in the morning, we arrived at the Del Moro swing station just as the light faded. I had wired ahead to O'Bannion to expect me, but was more than a little disturbed to find the old Irishman waiting for us there. I could tell from his face that something was badly wrong, certainly bad enough to drag him all the way from Dry Water in the livery's ramshackle buggy. Over coffee, I introduced Benbow as Kathleen Riley's associate from San Antonio and told him of his purpose in Dry Water, adding that I believed Hector Dulles would not object.

'He's not in too much of a position to object, Santana, that's why I'm here to meet you. Didn't want you riding into town so's they could blindside you.'

'Problems, Red?'

'They beat on old Hector pretty hard. Doc's got him at his place. He'll pull through OK, but it was touch and go there for a while. Same with your dog. Cream put a round in him, but Doc took care of him also. He'll walk with a limp and may have trouble cocking his leg to take a piss, but like Hector, he's pretty tough.'

'Jesus, Red, what happened here?' Every inch of my being wanted to be on the move, but O'Bannion was right, as was Benbow, in their urging that I listen and think the thing through.

'My guess is they followed you to Hector's place one time or other and when the eagles you so lavishly spread around the place began to turn up, Doyle figured you had found the Mother Lode, tried to make the old man spill his guts, but he took the beating quietly and never said a word.'

'Did they find the cave?'

'Yes, but obviously no gold and that's why they figure you have it; you found it and you cleared it out. Doyle's fit to bust, damned near lost his mind, acting like a crazy man. Wrecked the *Bugle*'s office and him, Cream and his five gunsels in black have the town treed.'

'The deputy?'

'Gone fishing.'

'That makes seven, assuming Doyle will want to play out the hand himself. You think they will calm down, maybe ride away?'

'Not likely, they have gone a tad too far to turn back now.'

'Where are they holed up?'

'They spend most of their time in the Cattlemen's, took over the whole top floor, turned your room over good.'

I turned to Benbow. 'What do you think, Jacob?'

'Your call, boss. I'll back your play whatever it is, as Beaufort would if he was here.'

'Too late to send for help, but of course we could just walk away and leave them be.' I looked at O'Bannion for a reaction to that idea.

'Hell no, they are drinking all of my liquor, already shot out that damned mirror I had shipped in from Dallas. Hell, I don't really give a shit for the

Tavern, but we can't leave Doc, Hector and the town to men like that.'

I signalled the barkeep for three fresh beers and tried to think it through, long-term through that is, cause and effect, the aftermath — as there was sure to be some killing on one side or the other.

'We can count on Jerry, Jackson the livery owner and some of the other businessmen to help if you show the way, Santana.'

'You cannot send businessmen up against the likes of Elmore Cream and we can't go charging in guns blazing. This isn't 1861, Dry Water isn't Tombstone and I'm not Wyatt Earp. We have no author-ity to back us if things go wrong.'

'Yes, you do have,' O'Bannion said quietly. 'I cannot do anything about the deputy. Max Hadley was the elected county sheriff's appointment. But before we were worthy of a deputy we had a town marshal and that's a town council appointment. And as of right now, I am the town council.'

'So where does that get us?' I asked.

O'Bannion's face reddened even more than usual as he fished inside his coat pocket and brought out a dull metal badge, a simple five-pointed star with the words Town Marshal and Dry Water Creek stamped into it. 'I brought this along just in case you would be of a mind to wearing it.'

'You really did kiss the Blarney Stone didn't you, O'Bannion?' I shook my head and smiled.

'You've actually heard of the Blarney Stone then, Santana?'

'You know I'm well-read.'

'You tell me that often enough, but will you wear this?'

I held out my hand and he dropped the badge gently on to my palm. 'Against my better judgement, but I guess it makes anything we do legal within reason.' I removed my gunbelt from my warbag and pinned the badge to the black leather, just in front of the holster.

'You're not going to wear it?' O'Bannion asked.

'Hell no, too much of a target.' I

turned to the smiling Jacob Benbow. 'You want to be my deputy, kid? No badge, but O'Bannion's word is good.'

'It needs to be. Two against seven — you had better come up with a good plan.'

'I'll think of one directly,' I said, hoping that I could.

* * *

At first light the next day with a good breakfast under our belts, we took the dusty trail back to Dry Water. The sky was a clear light blue, with just a hint of a cloud on a distant horizon. O'Bannion had brought the Morgan tied off behind the buggy and Benbow hired a mount from the Del Moro livery. We rode three abreast wherever the buggy made it possible for us to do so, which helped to avoid eating each other's dust. My plan, such as it was, was dictated by the options open to us. No way we could face down seven men and hope to walk away. And I did fully

214

intend to walk away, so it was to be a battle of attrition. Taking them down one at a time, from ambush if necessary, but if possible offering each the choice of walking away. Cream would shoot it out and Doyle, if he really had gone crazy, would also dig in; he had a lot to lose if it went against him, but the stink of gold is a powerful smell in the nostrils of a hungry man. The key to the whole thing was the Cattlemen's Hotel. Getting them out of there and separated was not going to be easy, but I had a plan for that as well. It involved the kid from the stable, O'Bannion's Blarney Stone blessed mouth and a couple or so of the double eagles I had retained as my share of the $1000 I had retrieved from the cave.

*   *   *

The plan went like this: A kid walks into the Bullhorn Cantina and asks for a sarsaparilla. It's a hot midday, so Cherry Vargas takes pity on the kid and pours him the drink and the kid pays him with a 20-$ gold piece for a ten-cent drink. While he is making change, Vargas asks him where he got the coin and the kid tells him some crazy guy is giving them away over at the livery stable. At about the same time, O'Bannion goes into Doyle's bank and deposits four gold pieces, and when the manager Harry Ballinger queries the source of the coins, O'Bannion tells him some crazy man down at the Overland office has a bucket full of them and is handing them like they were candy sticks.

Over the years, some lean and hungry years when a few bucks meant three square meals a day and shelter from life's unpredictable storms, I have learned that some things are predictable. And one is that if you throw money around, folk want to know where it came from. Another is that when a lot of money is being thrown around, people act before they think. Those two things were the basis of my hastily conceived plan. But, mostly, the idea was born of the certain knowledge that, other than with very rare exceptions, the greater majority of outlaws, thieves and all-around gunmen are not blessed with a great deal of intelligence — and even those excepted few were prone to act on impulse. I was counting on that fact with my life and the life of Jacob Benbow.

We left our horses below the creek and made our way to Dry Water quietly on foot well before sunrise, and while O'Bannion returned to the Tavern, Benbow and I chose our positions with some care.

I waited on the roof of the Overland stage depot with the Tavern's sawed-off 16 gauge shotgun I had borrowed from O'Bannion, while Benbow stationed himself deep in the shadows of the livery stable with a full sixteen rounds in the tubular magazine of his Henry rifle.

I watched as a hatless Ballinger walked swiftly across Main Street and entered the Cattlemen's Hotel. Within minutes, he was back on the street and into the bank, ushering customers out and closing the door behind them and seconds later hanging the closed sign on the barred glass door. I switched my attention to the Cantina; the kid was emerging looking at a handful of silver dollars and small change. He paused, selected a coin and pocketed the rest before heading for the general store and the candy counter where he'd been instructed to stay until told otherwise.

All pretty much predictable.

★   ★   ★

The hazy sun was well clear of the horizon and I didn't have too long to wait before two men in their black dusters emerged from the hotel and made their way toward the stage depot. I double-checked the shotgun shells and waited with both hammers cocked, alert to the fact that a third man had appeared on the street from the back entrance of the Bullhorn Cantina and was headed toward the livery stable.

Question in my mind was were the two men headed my way under orders from Doyle or were they just keen hound dogs, over-eager to bring him my bones. Almost certainly the Cantina gunman was acting alone as I had not seen Vargas leave the hotel. So three out of seven were in the open and I reckoned that the sound of imminent gunfire from either me or Benbow would shake a few more leaves from the tree.

The pair headed my way reached the depot ahead of the lone gunman making his way to the inviting wide open doors of the livery stable. They paused, got some distance between them and drew their revolvers, one moving slightly ahead of the other. I felt no pity for them; they were hired killers and would do me in at the drop of a hat, yet still it was not in me to gun them down without warning.

'Drop the irons, boys, and go belly down.'

I whispered the words, but they heard clearly enough and both chose to shoot it out, but it wasn't much of a contest. I gave them a single barrel each and wondered at the way they were both blown across the street, one leaving a half boot upright where he had last been standing. Neither man moved and they died as they had lived, in a silence known only to such a killer breed, guns for hire, men without pity. My death would not have troubled them as, on many a dark night, on a campfire-shadowed trail, theirs would impact upon me.

I shook these thoughts from my mind as I slid down behind the false front of the depot and made my way swiftly down to ground level, just as three quick rounds unmistakeably fired from a Henry rifle buffeted across the street. Benbow waved from the loft and quickly vanished from view. I gave him a minute to make the ground and ran along the rear of the Main Street buildings, past the *Bugle*'s office and the Green Frog Café, finally stationing myself at the rear of the Cattlemen's Hotel, hoping he was doing the same and keeping pace with me on the opposite side of the street and watching the front. In such situations it is of vital importance you know where your friends are. The odds were now better; I figured two to one as I did not believe Doyle would get into the fight — too fat, too clever to risk his own life. Cream was the main target. Chances were if he went down and Doyle refused to fight, the two remaining gunmen would quit and run. Standing there thinking of my next move, and knowing that Benbow would not make his move until he was certain it would be an action of which I would approve, was frustrating. He was calm under fire that boy, never known to make a hurried move without giving it considerable thought, and he was, could be, very inventive. He had been that way in Del Rio when Beaufort and I were pinned down by men who very much wanted us dead. Benbow had come down the street dressed in an overly long cloak, wearing dark glasses and tapping the ground in front of him with a white stick he had borrowed from a blind man in the local cantina. The distraction worked and attention was temporarily diverted from us and we made our way to a safer place, from which we sallied forth and shot our way clear. Meanwhile Benbow walked right on past us and the opposition, without once giving any sign that he was anything other than what he appeared to be. At the end of the street when the shooting started he had turned, swung his Henry out from under the cloak and joined the gunfight, still wearing the dark glasses.

But that was then, this was now.

Then came the shots: one, two, three, a pause. And then one, two, three, and another pause. I guessed it was Benbow. He was a marksman, and had probably found some safe cover and was raking the upper floor of the Cattlemen's Hotel, and with each pause he was feeding fresh shells into the tubular magazine of the Henry. If he had enough ammo and could keep it up all afternoon, sooner or later wherever they hid, whatever shelter they might find, a hit was likely and that would not please Doyle. But it continued: one, two, three, pause; one, two, three, pause. The door at the top of the outside back stairs cracked open and I waited but not for long. One, two, three, four, five, six, pause. Those extra three rounds seemed to convince the man behind the door that it was to time to get gone and he did just that, black duster flying, followed closely by a second man. They hit the stairs and I dropped the both of them without the customary warning. I was sick of it and wanted it over. It could have ended there, but it didn't.

'You out there, Santana, I want to talk . . . '

It was Doyle, but his words were cut short.

'No he doesn't, Santana, but I do.' It was Elmore Cream. 'In the street, just you and me, what do you say, you got the guts for that? *Mano a mano*, no posse, just you and me.'

He was shouting from the front of the hotel, assuming I was behind the gun shredding the hotel. I walked down the alleyway and out into the street, and stood there waiting, my presence his answer.

He came to the double doors, peered out into the sunlight, cautiously crossed the sidewalk and stepped down onto the rutted street, the long duster folded back behind his holstered Colt. He stared at me. 'Just who the fuck are you, Santana?'

'Very likely the last man you will ever see, Elmore Cream.'

'I don't believe so,' he said, and pulled.

This time around he was fast. He was prepared and a whole lot faster than he had been when I drew on him that time out at Purgatory, but it was still not fast enough and I shot him twice in the chest before he could drop the hammer. He twisted around almost full circle and fell face down. I walked over to him, kicked his fallen pistol clear and rolled him over with my boot. Sightless eyes staring up at I knew not what.

'He was a good man, Santana, a good

friend.' It was Doyle standing in the doorway, his weight taken on his black cane, his huge body covered in a dirty sweat-stained white suit, like some gargantuan parody of an illustration from *Moby Dick*. Like I said, I am sometimes too well-read.

'Is he dead?' There was a genuine sadness in the question to which he already knew the answer.

I holstered my Colt as he stepped forward and raised the cane, and just too late I remembered that O'Bannion had warned me it was a 4.10 shotgun. But in that same instant the unmistakeable roar of a shotgun, the blast tossing the big man backwards and down onto his backside. As he fell, the end of the cane belched flame and the wayward ball buried itself at my feet. Daniel Doyle sat there upright, his eyes watering and dying in that position, fading away into that big darkness, taking the same endless ride as his man Elmore Cream.

O'Bannion was at my side, a smoking shotgun in his shaking hands. I gently removed it from him, broke the gun and shucked the remaining shell on to the street. 'Thanks,' I said quietly.

'One time he wasn't all bad, Santana. We had our moments. God, Ireland is so long ago and so far away.' I put my arm around his shoulder, nodded my thanks to Jacob Benbow, who had emerged from a building opposite the hotel, and led the trembling old Irishman back to the Green Frog and Molly who was running towards us.

* * *

Mid-morning and I was standing outside of the tavern with O'Bannion, Molly, Hector and Bart, waiting for Jacob Benbow to bring by our horses from the livery stable. My warbag and saddle-bag were packed and I was anxious to be on my way. I turned as Max Hadley approached. It was the first I had seen of the man since the gunfight a week earlier.

'You thinking of going somewheres, Santana?'

Max Hadley was a big man and I had no intention whatsoever in brawling with him. He could hurt me and I could hurt my hands on his large jaw; in either case, something to be avoided.

'I'm leaving town, deputy, no need for you to crowd me. I want as much gone between us as you do. Sheriff Murdock has my report as both a Pinkerton man and Dry Water's town marshal. I guess you are about to lose your job. Don't make it worse with a felonious assault charge to boot.'

I could see he wasn't interested in anything I had to say. He moved toward me, a pair of irons dangling from his big hand.

'Felonious assault, what the hell is that?'

'You tell me, you're the lawman.'

'Shut your smart mouth, Santana, unbuckle that gunbelt and put these on. I'm not wearing a gun, so you pulling on me now with these people watching would be a mistake. You are the one going to jail, whether it be for the

227

murder of Danny Doyle or an assault on me is up to you.'

'That doesn't make any sense,' I said. 'The US Marshal and the circuit judge were just here and they cleared me of any wrongdoing.'

'I'm not going to ask you again, Santana.'

He stepped closer, a mistake an experienced badge would never have made. I kicked him hard on the right leg, heard the bone crack as I reached into my hip pocket, pulled out the leaded sap I sometimes carried for just such occasions and hit him hard across the temple. His eyes rolled up into his skull and he pitched forward into my open arms. I gently lowered him the boardwalk and, reaching down, ripped the star from his vest and tossed it to O'Bannion.

'He was no lawman, Red, and does not deserve to wear the badge. He will have a headache, but he will come round. Do your best to stop him riding my back trail, in fact lock him up in his jail until Murdock gets here.'

He grinned. 'Be a pleasure. You keep in touch now, you hear?'

'Will do, and thanks.'

Benbow and I rode slowly down Dry Water's Main Street, followed by a limping Black Bart, headed for San Antonio, the railhead there and the long journey home to Wyoming. Of the few people gathered in the street, only the O'Bannions and the recovering Hector Dulles waved. I guessed the rest were more than happy to see the back of the Peaceful River Kid, but I had a weird feeling that I had not seen the last of Max Hadley.

16

Wyoming, My Own Sweet Home

I was standing by the log pile brushing down the Morgan when Gus Street rode into the front yard, close by to where Annie was weeding her rose bed. Bart was at her side as was usual. He had adopted her, having found her to be more susceptible to his dark eyes and hungry look than ever I had been.

Gus shook my hand and nodded toward where Annie was working. She looked up and waved but did not join us. 'Where did you steal the mutt? Ugly sonofabtich.'

'He rightly is a son of a bitch, Gus, but best mind your mouth. He's a West Texas dog and is likely to be packing. You put on a bit of weight, old man, likely you will soon need a bigger horse and I can have that mare.'

'I see you already got a new Morgan.'

'She's West Texas as well, so don't walk behind her.'

I had been back at Wildcat for maybe a week and it was the first visit from the lawman, him being busy as it was election year and he had flesh to press and fundraiser engagements to cover.

He sighed, his face clouded, he dipped the tin cup in the water bucket hanging on the branch above my head and took a deep swallow. I could see he was in no mind for banter. 'You get into any fracas down south this trip, Lucas?'

'Nothing worth mentioning,' I lied. I was becoming a good liar if there is such a person.

'I got a wire from a sheriff down there in Dry Water, name of Hadley. Says you are wanted in his county for aggravated and felonious assault, whatever the hell that is, and murder. Want to tell me about it?'

'Felonious assault? Never heard of such a dumb thing either and I have nothing to say, your honour. Whatever

231

it was, I didn't do it, but I am often mistaken for someone else,' I said solemnly, kicking the dust with my boot and taking on a hangdog look. 'Shucks, sheriff, 'tweren't my fault, no siree bub, not my doin' at all. Damned thing just went off in my hand.'

'Ok, you can cut out the good ol' boy peckerwood act, but I have to answer it. He's an elected official; we cooperate county to county, even if not state by state in these enlightened times.' Pondering about that thought, he added. 'The state went to the crapper when they gave women the vote back in '69. You can't hardly spit on the sidewalk now without causing a big howtodo.' He took out his pipe and filled it, tamped the tobacco down and waited patiently.

'Seriously, Gus, first off, he was a two-bit ex-deputy, since fired, working in a remote cow town called Dry Water. Some nice folk there but it's still a dusty crap hole. Secondly, he objected to me wearing my gun on the outside of my pants. In Texas of all places, would you believe that?'

'Hard to believe it of Texas.' That face-splitting smile; we both had a kind of love-hate relationship with the Lone Star State.

'He tried to take it from me one last time before I left town. He is one big old boy, but I decked him with that sap you gave me. That was it. Me, the Morgan, a Pinkerton agent named Benbow and old Bart there were on the trail to San Antonio and gone, headed for home long before he woke up from that slap stick of yours.' I looked up at the house and said quietly, 'Between you and me, Gus, I may well be going back there one of these days. May have some unfinished business down there.'

'The murder?'

'A gunfight, a bunch of yahoos and a corrupt rancher, self-defence. I was behind a town marshal's badge and US Marshal Beaudine cleared that charge, as did the circuit judge.'

'That it?'

I nodded. 'That's it.'

'Bullshit bit of paper,' he said. 'I thought it might be.'

'Something else bothering you, Gus?'

'Yes, the wolvers. Briggs and his crew hit town a few days back. They seem pretty worked up and cocky about something. Maybe it's nothing. Maybe it will just catch the wind and blow away when they have spent their pokes. But if not, remember I am the law in Peaceful and I will back you should you need me.' He smiled at me then, his voice softening, business over and done with, two lawmen sitting in the sun. 'You and Annie coming to the dance on Saturday? It's a fundraiser for the new church. You being a religious man and all, thought you might like to join us. Maybe give me a chance to dance with that pretty wife of yours, show her a few moves we old-timers can still make.'

17

On the Dark Edge of Nowhere

Annie and I rode into town on Saturday, booked into the Drover's Rest hotel, and ate a late lunch at the Chinaman's. That afternoon while Annie did some shopping I aimed to take laced coffee with Gus in his office. Only he wasn't in his office. He was face-down in the dust outside of the saloon, with the big wolver Briggs standing over him, a large Bowie knife in his hand, with two similarly-dressed tramps in stiff wolf skins standing a little ways behind him. Annie suddenly burst from the gathering crowd with a wild-eyed Doc Morris at her side. Gus was struggling to get to his feet, but together Morris and Annie pushed him back down just as I joined them.

'Old fart came at me,' Briggs said to no one in particular. 'I didn't see no badge.'

I looked at him, but said nothing and, with the help of Halloran and Morris, picked the old lawman up. Sharing his heavy weight between us, we carried him across to the sidewalk, through the gathering crowd and down along Main Street to the sheriff's office. We hefted him onto the wooden cot on which he sometimes overnighted and while Doc fussed over him, Annie Blue helped tear off the old man's shirt.

'Missed the artery, just,' Morris said, relief in his tired voice. 'He's bled some but he'll live, tough as old leather.' Gus looked up from the table, nodded to me and closed his eyes.

Jimmy Coltrane, the young part-time deputy, went to the gun rack and selected a carbine, but I stepped forward and gently took it from his trembling hands. The youngster looked at me, not sure whether to be resentful or simply relieved. I spared him the worry of that decision and slipped the carbine back into its slot, selected a double-barrelled sawed-off Colt 12-guage and filled my jacket pocket with double-ought buck shells from the ammo drawer beneath the racked long guns. 'Not your day, son. Get yourself a shotgun and just watch my back.'

He nodded. 'It's my job, sir.'

'Not today, Jerry. I brought that scum in to this town and it's my job to clear him out.'

'You got no badge, the county pays me to . . .'

I turned my back on him and walked over to the desk, opened the drawer and took out the leather wallet Kathleen Riley had insisted I take way back in South Texas and which I had given Gus for safe-keeping. I looked at that star cut into the nickel silver shield long and hard before removing it from the wallet and pinning it to my vest just over my heart, the perfect target, thinking this was the second time I had worked from behind a shield in the last four weeks. 'I'm making this federal, son. Gus was an elected peace officer so you just do as I ask and from here you watch that street and protect Gus and Annie if things go south.'

I had not worn my sidearm to town as there was never a need for it in Peaceful and I really did not expect any trouble from Briggs. I had seen him off once before and I felt I could do it again should it prove necessary. I had though, as an afterthought, strapped on the shoulder rig with its snubbed Colt .38 that once belonged to Darryl Jones of New Orleans and given me by the parish deputies who had pried him loose from the spare office chair. It was useful close up, but with its very short barrel not of much use in a street shootout should it come to that. Gus's gun-belt would have gone around my waist twice and I was not happy with the spare office leather, so I lifted his .45 Colt Army clear, checked the loads, added a sixth round to the one empty chamber he always carried under the hammer and stuck the piece in the waistband of my pants, nestled it down in the small of my back.

Doc Morris was fussing over the

sheriff who had lapsed into sleep, helped along by the laudanum he had administered.

'I'll be going, Doc. You OK here?'

'Get it done, Santana.' He did not look up from his chore.

I took out two shotgun shells from my pocket, shook them to ensure they were charged and slipped them into the short-barrelled sawed-off, touched Annie's arm gently and walked to the door. She nodded and gave me a sad smile. Teton Sioux women are not given to tears when their men go to war; they know their man has to walk in his own shadow, and knowing that is enough for the both of them.

* * *

Main Street was deserted, the way they always are before a gunfight. Word travels fast and so do stray bullets. I stood there thinking it through. I could see Bart hiding under the far boardwalk, but not another living soul.

'Two of 'em are in Halloran's Saloon. They treed the place. The one did the knifing, I don't know.' The voice was a whisper from the shadow of the alley. Wade Thomas, owner of the general store, an old hand and member of the Saturday night poker school, along with me, Gus and Mark Halloran. 'I've got a sixteen gauge loaded for bear. You need me, holler.'

'Stay clear, Wade; these are hard men not wayward cowhands. But thanks anyway. I've got Jerry watching my back. And however it goes down, you leave the big man to me; it's an old score.'

'You look good behind that badge, Lucas, but I'm here anyway and I got nothing else to do.'

I stepped out into the street and made my slow way over to Halloran's then, turning away from the swing doors, I ducked down the alleyway and up the outside stairway, much travelled by the townsmen and ranch hands that frequented the bedrooms there when the ladies of the carnival or the rodeo were in town. Peaceful sure was a liberal place; I could not help but smile at the thought.

I climbed through the nearest open window, tiptoed across the room, gently opened the door and stepped out onto the railed gallery, my back pressed to the wall, looking down onto the silent room. Two of the wolvers were at the bar drinking from bottles. They each carried a firearm, one a sixteen-shot Henry and the other a full length 12-guage. Customers were huddled into one corner of the room, but Halloran was still behind the bar. He knew I would be coming and where I would be coming from. Mark Halloran was an old time lawman from Kansas, now rotund and red of face, whose arthritic hands had long ago robbed him of his badge but not of his awareness to any threatening confrontation.

I knew he had seen me, although he gave no indication of that fact. I propped the shotgun against the wall and drew Street's long Colt; too many customers in the saloon to risk a spread of heavy buckshot.

One of the two men lifted a half full bottle to his lips, took a long pull then spat it out, turning to Halloran and saying, 'Forty-rod rotgut. Break out the real stuff, you tired old windbag, before I put you down.'

He waved the long gun in Halloran's direction, just as I stepped clear of the wall, fanning the hammer of the big six. He bounced across the room like he had been kicked by a mule, ricocheted off the bar and back into a table, then onto the saw-dusted board floor. His companion stood frozen for a second and then loosed the Henry at me, working the lever as fast as he could, the wild bullets splintering the wood-work all around me. I fired twice and hit him, but not hard enough to drop him. Still firing, he made it to the swing doors and stepped out into the street, seconds later flying back through the entrance as four loads of heavy buck-shot, I guessed fired from the shotguns of both the young deputy and Wade Thomas, sent him to his maker.

I made my way to the bottom of the stairs and nodded to Halloran, who poured a shot and slid it along the bar to me. I lifted it and swallowed it, before turning to the frightened customers who had just witnessed two men being blown to kingdom come.

I set the hot Colt on the bar. 'I'm empty, Mark. You got any .45 ammo?'

He shook his head and surveyed the frightened faces of the customers who had just come out for a quiet Saturday afternoon's drink. 'People don't pack much these days, Lucas. Gus keeps a tight lid on the town. Not much need to carry a firearm anymore.'

'True enough.' I looked around at the worried faces. 'A round of drinks on the county, Mr Halloran, and make sure they stay put until this thing is done.'

Then the hard rasping voice of the wolver Briggs. 'I'm waiting on you, cat lover, and I'm not waiting all day. I got me some more killing to do, maybe sparkin' with your squaw woman, you goddamned crazy Indian lover.'

One thing you learn very quickly if you really want to be a shootist and survive is never to allow your adversary to rile you. All too often a gunfight is won not by the fastest man to pull but by the coolest man. Likely you only get the one shot and that has to count. A fast gun firing three rounds that miss may look pretty fancy, but not so fancy if you end up on your back looking up through a third eye at a sky full of nothing.

Briggs' words had no effect on me whatsoever. But I did have a plan, having no intention whatsoever of dying under his gun that day in Peaceful. I checked the five loads in the .38, shucked the rounds out of the shotgun, snapped the breach closed. I cocked both hammers, though, and stepped out into the early afternoon sunshine, knowing I needed an edge.

Briggs was standing halfway across and down the street, facing the saloon and a little out of effective range of the sawed-off. He carried what looked to be a double action Smith and Wesson .38 and its six-inch barrel was pointed at me.

'Where's my goddamned Sharps, you thieving sono-fabitch?'

I did not answer, but tilted the 12-gauge and pulled both triggers. The loud clicks as the hammers hit the firing pins sounded like thunder in that quiet street. Briggs laughed briefly distracted. 'That all you got, no fancy six gun?'

'Not today,' I said quietly and ran directly at him, pulling the late departed Jonesy's snubbed Colt from the shoulder holster as I ran and, holding the trigger back, fanned four shots at him in quick succession. Considering the short barrel, my running and the closing distance between us, it was pretty fancy shooting. Briggs staggered backwards across the street twisting as each of the light rounds struck him, his Smith getting off a single round that hit me hard in the thigh. His last twist hung him over the hitching rail in front of the bank. I limped over to him, my left boot filling with blood, and fired the last round into the back of his shaggy head. He hung there perfectly balanced until gravity took over and he slid back into the street. His last contact with the rail was his open jaw hitting the wood, snapping it forever shut. He stared up at me, his eyes in the ruined face dimming as he wandered off into the big darkness, a darkness that was rapidly consuming me.

I tried walking, but my legs would not propel me forwards. I dropped the hot Colt and sank down onto my knees, staying there on all fours, waiting for the darkness, knowing it was coming and fighting it, hovering on the dark edge of the big nowhere, then seeing a small gleam of light as hands supported me. Bart licking my face, Annie holding me, Doc tying something tight around my leg, Halloran and Thomas and the young deputy carrying me toward the light, out of the valley of the shadow of death and into the soft grey light of sleep from which I somehow knew I would eventually awaken.

Epilogue

I arose early in the morning, a full week following the gun-fight on Peaceful's Main Street, and favouring my wounded leg, saddled the Morgan and made the gentle ride up to Willard's Rocks at the base of our small mountain, close by to where I had buried the cat I had foolishly named Cleopatra. I dismounted, ground-hitched the mare and settled my backside on a warm flat rock. The valley below me was at peace with itself. The aspens were turning to red and gold and the inevitable late fall Wyoming breeze gently, slowly and with great care began to strip them of their autumn leaves. The buffalo were gone and now only a distant memory, the wolf and the cougar, killed or chased to higher ground along the distant Yellowstone and the Big Horn Mountains. I wondered would we ever see their like again. I rolled a cigarette but did not light it. I watched as a small covey of partridge burst from the brush disturbed by an oncoming rider and was happy to see Annie Blue on her pinto, picnic bundle and blanket tied to her cantle. She paused by the Morgan, slid from the saddle, untucked her yellow skirt from the top of her drawers and, shaking out the wrinkles, made her way over to me.

'Hi, lonesome. You want some company? I brought grub and lemonade.'

'You bring any beer?' I asked smiling, pleased to see her.

'No beer. You lost a heck of a lot of blood and Doc says you need fluids.'

'Beer is fluids,' I said.

She ignored me. 'But I did stop by that old sink hole below the ford, filled the canteen for your horse in case she needed it. I saw some fresh cat tracks there — small, perhaps a young one,' she said gently, adding, 'Maybe it will stay.'

I felt a little flush of joy, and looked past her and down into valley across the gently-moving grass to where a hint of smoke from our stove tempted the breeze.

'That would be fine, Annie. It will be good to have a lion back on our mountain.'

She looked at me long and hard, reached out and took my hand and following my gaze said quietly, 'I do believe it already has one, Lucas, but there is room enough for two.'

She whispered the words almost as if to herself. I stared at her, the meaning of her thoughts lost to me.

We do hope that you have enjoyed
reading this large print book.

Did you know that all of our titles
are available for purchase?

We publish a wide range of high
quality large print books including:
Romances, Mysteries, Classics
General Fiction
Non Fiction and Westerns

Special interest titles available in
large print are:
The Little Oxford Dictionary
Music Book, Song Book
Hymn Book, Service Book

Also available from us courtesy of
Oxford University Press:
Young Readers' Dictionary
(large print edition)
Young Readers' Thesaurus
(large print edition)

For further information or a free
brochure, please contact us at:
Ulverscroft Large Print Books Ltd.,
The Green, Bradgate Road, Anstey,
Leicester, LE7 7FU, England.
Tel: (00 44) **0116 236 4325**
Fax: (00 44) **0116 234 0205**